The Watcher was mounted on a huge rock. Harkins saw a man, or something like a man, with gray-green, rugose skin, pale, sightless eyes, and tiny, dangling boneless arms. Its mouth was wide and grotesque, contorted into something possibly intended to be a grin.

"We must talk," the Watcher said.

Harkins stared in awe and surprise. "Who are you? What are you doing here?"

The thick lips writhed in a terrifying smirk. "No, young man, the question is what are *you* doing here."

"Well, why am I here?" Harkins said uneasily.

"You?" The Watcher laughed coldly. "Why, you're the random factor in a two-thousand-year-old chess game. . . ."

—From the fantastic novella,
"Slaves of the Star Giants"

NEXT STOP
THE STARS

by

ROBERT SILVERBERG

ace books
A Division of Charter Communications Inc.
A GROSSET & DUNLAP COMPANY
1120 Avenue of the Americas
New York, New York 10036

NEXT STOP THE STARS

TABLE OF CONTENTS

NEXT STOP THE STARS

Introduction

NEXT STOP THE STARS was the first collection of my short stories to be published, and holds a special place in my affections for that reason. By now my collected short stories run to sixteen or seventeen volumes, and some of those volumes are a good deal more impressive than this one; but first is first, and first things never lose their significance. Besides, it's an interesting book in its own right, for a lot of reasons.

The thing about short story collections is that they generally don't sell as well as novels, unless the author is someone who is primarily known only for short stories—as, for example, Ray Bradbury. Story collections are usually awarded by publishers as bribes, or, shall we say, sweeteners, to writers whose good will they wish to earn. The theory is that if you let a writer bring out a volume of his collected short stories, you may also be able to get him to let you have one of his novels.

Circa 1957, when I first tried to interest a publisher in doing a book of my short stories, no one was especially interested in earning my good will in that fashion. I was a promising young writer—indeed, I had in 1956 been awarded a Hugo as Most Promising New Writer—and I had sold a whole raft of stories and novels, some of them pretty good, some awful; but I was still operating very much in a buyer's market for my work. I had the feeling common to most young writers that whatever I managed to get published was making its way into print mainly because the editor had a certain number of blank pages to fill every month, and what I was writing was decent enough to make the minimum grade in the absence of anything better. That is to say, if Heinlein or Sturgeon or Leiber or Asimov had bothered to turn in a story that month, I'd have been out, but they didn't and so I racked up another sale. On the other hand, I also had the feeling common to most young writers that some of what I was writing was pretty good, maybe even as good as the stuff that the really bigtime authors were producing, and deserved the immortality of a book edition just as much as anything they had produced. Since *they* were having shortstory collections published, I put together one of my own. I don't now remember what it was called, but it contained ten or twelve of the best stories I had written in the three or four years of my career. I shipped it down to my agent with the usual high hopes.

The problem was that my books were then being published by Ace, and Ace didn't do short story collections. So the collection had to be offered to houses like Ballantine and Doubleday, which did collections only as sweeteners for their regular novelists, of whom I was not then one. So there was no sale, and I looked ruefully at the other writers' collections with feelings of envy and sorrow.

Eventually Ace did start doing collections—the first, an Eric Frank Russell volume, appeared in

1958—and I began hinting to the Ace editor, Donald Wollheim, that I would appreciate one myself. The Ace system was a bit different from that of other publishers: instead of doing a separate volume of short stories, Ace tacked the collection to a novel by the same author, doing both works in one binding in the celebrated Ace Double format. That wasn't quite as satisfying to the author as a single book of his stories would have been, but it was much less risky for the publisher, and at least the author had the satisfaction of having an entire Ace Double to himself.

I hinted, but Wollheim didn't seem to get the hint, and I went uncollected for another couple of years. Late in 1961 Ace acquired a book of mine called THE SEED OF EARTH, the complex history of which is recounted in the new edition issued as a companion to this present volume. And—with a little nudge from my agent—Don finally agreed to do a Silverberg story collection as the flip half of the double volume.

Hastily I unearthed my unsold collection of 1957. I picked the four best stories from it, and added to them a novella, "Slaves of the Star Giants," that had not been included in the original group. The main reason for the substitution was that Ace, back then, preferred strong, colorful, action-oriented adventure stories, and none of the short stories in my original story collection quite qualified as that. "Star Giants" did. It had been written for the first issue of an ephemeral magazine called *Science Fiction Adventures*, and it was an appropriately colorful job, decorated with mutants, giant aliens, mad robots, and other such equipment. It gave the book a certain solidity, even though it wasn't exactly what I considered an ideal kind of science fiction.

The four short stories appended to it, though, were something else again. In their various ways they represented the young Silverberg at his best, striving to master the difficult art of the science fiction short story.

Oldest of them was "Hopper," written in June of 1954, when I was in my sophomore year at college. Here we see an early try at the time-paradox plot, to which I would return throughout my career; here also are decent attempts at characterization, style, and creation of a plausible future society. I thought it was quite a mature story for a writer not yet out of his teens, and still do; and I was much wounded when "Hopper" failed to sell to *Astounding*, *Galaxy*, or any of the other leading magazines of the time. (It finally published in Larry Shaw's superb, much underrated magazine, *Infinity*, two years after I wrote it. Years later I expanded it into a novel, *The Time Hoppers*, for Doubleday.)

In June of 1955, while still an undergraduate, I wrote "The Songs of Summer"—an extremely ambitious technical stunt, an attempt at telling a story through a series of fragmented monologs. I thought it came off quite well, but again the important magazines chose to turn it down, and after a year in the wilderness the story was purchased by my friend Robert W. Lowndes for his *Science Fiction Stories*, a magazine that managed a surprising level of excellence even though its word rates were the lowest in the field.

You can imagine, I think, the discouraging effect on a young writer to have stories of this caliber go begging for a home for a year or more. I think that had "Hopper" and "Songs of Summer" and my other ambitious stories of 1954 and 1955 found publishers when I wrote them, I would probably never have deviated into the attitudes that led me to write "Slaves of the Star Giants" and scores of other adventure stories. But none of those early good stories sold on their merits; they all got published eventually only because I had established working professional contacts with editors; and the cynicism that they engineered in me taught me a lesson I was years in unlearning, that is, that there was no sense in trying to do my best.

The remaining stories in the collection were written only a few years after the first two, but they come from an entirely different era. "Slaves of the Star Giants" dates from September, 1956. I was out of college then, already married, a Hugo winner, and an established professional author. No longer was I sending stories off into the void and hoping they would sell; I had demonstrated to editors that I could reliably supply them with publishable commodities, and they were *asking* me for stories, generally of a certain length to be delivered by a certain date. "Star Giants" was such an assigned story. I remember writing it in the first weeks of my marriage, on a folding table in the cavernous, still almost unfurnished apartment we had rented on West End Avenue in Manhattan. No masterpiece, certainly, but its young author, certainly, was a pro.

And the other two date from 1957, when I was already growing restless doing adventure fiction and was trying to work my way back to the more serious s-f I had set out originally to write in 1954. "Warm

Man," written in January, 1957, was my first sale to urbane and sophisticated Anthony Boucher of *Fantasy & Science Fiction*, and an appropriately urbane and sophisticated story it is, too, a far cry from the thud-and-blunder of "Star Giants." Later that same month I did "Blaze of Glory," a study in irony that has many points of resonance with my later fiction, and sold it to Horace L. Gold of *Galaxy*, probably the most demanding editor in the business, a man who constantly goaded me (with some belated success) to stretch my talents beyond their present reach.

Not a bad group of stories for a writer who was still in his very early twenties when the last of them was written. I was much excited when they finally appeared in collected form in 1962 as half of Ace Double Book F-145, with my novel THE SEED OF EARTH on the other side. NEXT STOP THE STARS was given a striking cover painting by Ed Emsh, SEED OF EARTH a less impressive but still attractive illustration, perhaps by Ed Valigursky, making for a pleasant little package.

Robert Silverberg
Oakland, California
April, 1976

SLAVES OF THE STAR GIANTS

CHAPTER I

DARK VIOLET shadows streaked the sky, and the forest was ugly and menacing. Lloyd Harkins leaned against the bole of a mighty red-brown tree and looked around dizzily, trying to get his bearings.

He knew he was *there*, not *here*. *Here* had vanished, so suddenly that there had been no sense of transition or of motion—merely a strange subliminal undertone of *loss*, as the world he knew had melted and been replaced with—what?

He heard a distant, ground-shaking sound of thunder, growing louder. Birds with gleaming, toothy beaks and wide-sweeping wings wheeled and shrieked in the shadowed sky, and the air was cold and damp. Harkins held his ground, clinging tightly to the enormous tree as if it were his last bastion of reality in a world of dreams.

And the tree moved.

It lifted from its base, swung forward and upward, carrying Harkins with it. The sound of thunder grew nearer. Harkins shut his eyes, opened them, gaped in awe.

Some ten feet to the right, another tree was moving.

He threw his head back, stared upward into the cloud-fogged sky, and verified the fact he wanted to deny: the trees were not trees.

They were legs.

Legs of a being huge beyond belief, whose head rose fifty feet or more above the floor of the dark forest. A being who had begun to move.

Harkins dug his hands frantically into the leg, gripping it as he swung wildly through a fifteen-foot arc with each stride of the monstrous creature. Gradually, the world around him took shape again, and slowly he re-established control over his fear-frozen mind.

Through the bright green blurs of vegetation he was able to see the creature on which he rode. It was gigantic but vaguely manlike, wearing a sort of jacket and a pair of shorts which terminated some twenty-five feet above Harkins' head. From there down, firm red-brown skin the texture of wood was visible. Harkins could even distinguish dimly a face, far above, with pronounced features of a strange and alien cast.

He began to assemble his environment. It was a forest—where? On Earth, apparently—but an Earth no one had ever known before. The bowl of the sky was shot through with rich, dark colors, and the birds that screeched overhead were nightmare creatures of terrifying appearance.

The earth was brown and the vegetation green, though all else had changed.

Where am I? Harkins asked over and over again.

And—*Why am I here?*

And—*How can I get back?*

He had no answers. The day had begun in ordinary fashion, promising to be neither more nor less unusual than the day before or all the days before that. Shortly after noon, on the 21st of April, 1957, he had been on his way to the electronics laboratory, in New York City, on the planet Earth. And now he was here, wherever *here* might be.

His host continued to stride through the forest, seemingly unconcerned about the man clinging to his calf. Harkins' arms were growing tired from the strain of hanging on, and suddenly the new thought occurred: *Why not let go?* He had held on only through a sort of paralysis of the initiative, but now he had regained his mental equilibrium. He dropped off.

He hit the ground solidly and sprawled out flat. The soil was warm and fertile-smelling, and for a moment he clung to it as he had to the "tree" minutes before. Then he scrambled to his feet and glanced around hastily, looking for a place to hide and reconnoiter.

There was none. And a hand was descending toward him—red-brown, enormous, tipped with gleaming, pointed fingernails six inches long. Gently, the giant hand scooped Harkins up.

There was a dizzying moment as he rose fifty feet, held tenderly in the giant's leathery embrace. The hand opened, and Harkins found himself standing on an outspread palm the size of a large table, staring at a strange oval face with deep-set, compassionate eyes and a wide, almost lipless mouth studded with triangular teeth. The being seemed to smile almost pityingly at Harkins.

"What are you?" Harkins demanded.

The creature's smile grew broader and more melancholy, but there was no reply—only the harsh wailing of the forest birds, and the distant rumbling of approaching thunder. Harkins felt himself being lowered to the giant's side, and once again the being began to move rapidly through the forest, crushing down the low-clustered shrubs as it walked. Harkins, his stomach rolling agonizingly with each step, rode cradled in the great creature's loosely-closed hand.

After what must have been ten minutes or more, the giant stopped. Harkins glanced around, surprised. The thunder was close now, and superimposed on it was the dull boom of toppling trees. The giant was standing quite still, legs planted as solidly as tree trunks, waiting.

Minutes passed—and then Harkins saw why the giant had stopped. Coming toward them was a machine—a robot, Harkins realized—some fifteen feet high. It was man-shaped, but much more compact; a unicorn-like spike projected from its gleaming nickel-jacketed forehead, and instead of legs it moved on broad treads. The robot was proceeding through the forest, pushing aside the trees that stood in its way with casual gestures of its massive forearms, sending them toppling to the right and left with what looked like a minimal output of effort.

The giant remained motionless, staring down at the ugly machine as it went by. The robot paid no attention to Harkins' host, and went barrelling on through the forest as if following some predetermined course.

Minutes later it was out of sight leaving behind it a trail of uprooted shrubs and exposed tree-roots. As the robot's thunder diminished behind them, the giant resumed his journey through the forest. Harkins rode patiently, not daring to think any more.

After a while longer a clearing appeared—and Harkins was surprised and pleased to discover a little cluster of huts. Man-sized huts, ringed in a loose circle to form a village. Moving in the center of the circle were tiny dots which Harkins realized were people, human beings, men.

A colony?

A prison camp?

The people of the village spotted the giant, and gathered in a small knot, gesticulating and pointing. The giant approached within about a hundred yards of the village, stooped, and lowered Harkins delicately to the ground.

Dizzy after his long journey in the creature's hand, Harkins staggered, reeled, and fell. He half expected to see the giant scoop him up again, but instead the being was retreating into the forest, departing as mysteriously as he had come.

Harkins got to his feet. He saw people running toward him—wild-looking, dangerous people. Suddenly, he began to feel that he might have been safer in the giant's grip.

CHAPTER II

THERE WERE seven of them, five men and two wo-men. These were probably the bravest. The rest hung back and watched from the safety of their huts.

Harkins stood fast and waited for them. When they drew near, he held up a hand.

"Friend!" he said loudly. "Peace!"

The words seemed to register. The seven paused and arrayed themselves in an uneasy semicircle before Harkins. The biggest of the men, a tall, broad-shouldered man with unruly long black hair, thick features and deep-set eyes, stepped forward.

"Where are you from, stranger?" he growled in recognizable, though oddly distorted, English.

Harkins thought it over, and decided to keep acting on the assumption that they were as savage as they looked. He pointed to the forest. "From there."

"We know that," the tall man said. "We saw the Star Giant bring you. But where is your village?"

Harkins shrugged. "Far from here—far across the ocean." It was as good a story as any, he thought. And he wanted more information about these people before he volunteered any about himself. But one of the two women spoke up.

"What ocean?" Her voice was scornful. She was a

6

squat, yellow-faced woman in a torn, dirty tunic. "There are no oceans near here." She edged up to Harkins, glared intently at him. Her breath was foul. "You're a *spy*," she said accusingly. "You're from the Tunnel City, aren't you?"

"The Star Giant brought him," the other woman pointed out calmly. She was tall and wild-looking, with flowing blonde hair that looked as if it had never been cut. She wore ragged shorts and two strips of cloth that covered her breasts. "The Star Giants aren't in league with the city dwellers, Elsa," the woman added.

"Quiet," snapped the burly man who had spoken first. He turned to Harkins. "Who are you?"

"My name is Lloyd Harkins. I come from far across the ocean. I don't know how I came here, but the Star Giant"—this part would be true, at least—"found me and brought me to this place." He spread his hands. "More I cannot tell you."

"Uh. Very well, Lloyd Harkins." The big man turned to the other six. "Kill him, or let him stay?"

"How unlike you to ask our opinions, Jorn!" said the squat woman named Elsa. "But I say kill him. He's from the Tunnel City. I know it!"

The man named Jorn faced the others. "What say you?"

"Let him live," replied a sleepy-looking young man. "He seems harmless."

Jorn scowled. "The rest of you?"

"Death," said a second man. "He looks dishonest."

"He looks all right to me," offered the third.

"And to me," said the fourth. "But I vote for death. Elsa is seldom wrong."

7

Harkins chewed nervously at his lower lip. That made three votes for death, two in his favor. Jorn was staring expectantly at the sullen-faced girl with long hair.

"Your opinion, Katha?"

"Let him live," she said slowly.

Jorn grunted. "So be it. I cast my vote for him also. You may join us, stranger. But mine is the deciding vote—and if I reverse it, you die!"

They marched over the clearing single file to the village, Jorn leading, Harkins in the rear followed by the girl Katha. The rest of the villagers stared at him curiously as he entered the circle of huts.

"This is Lloyd Harkins," Jorn said loudly. "He will live among us."

Harkins glanced tensely from face to face. There were about seventy of them, altogether, ranging from gray-beards to naked children. They seemed oddly savage and civilized all at once. The village was a strange mixture of the primitive and cultured.

The huts were made of some unfamiliar dark green plastic substance, as were their clothes. A bonfire burnt in the center of the little square formed by the ring of huts. From where he stood, Harkins had a clear view of the jungle—a thickly-vegetated one, which had obviously not sprung up overnight. He could see the deeply-trampled path which the Star Giant had made.

He turned to Jorn. "I'm a stranger to this land. I don't know anything about the way you live."

"All you need to know is that I'm in charge," Jorn said. "Listen to me and you won't have any trouble."

"Where am I going to stay?"

"There's a hut for single men," Jorn said. "It's not very comfortable, but it's the best you can have." Jorn's deep eyes narrowed. "There are no spare women in this village, by the way. Unless you want Elsa, that is." He threw back his head and laughed raucously.

"Elsa's got her eyes fixed on one of the Star Giants," someone else said. "That's the only kind can satisfy her."

"*Toad!*" The squat woman known as Elsa sprang at the man who had spoken, and the ferocity of her assault knocked him to the ground. Elsa climbed on his chest and began banging his head against the ground. With a lazy motion, Jorn reached down and plucked her off.

"Save your energy, Elsa. We'll need you to cast spells when the Tunnel City men come."

Harkins frowned. "This Tunnel City—where is it? Who lives there?"

Jorn swung slowly around. "Either you're a simpleton or you really *are* a stranger here. The Tunnel City is one of the Old Places. Our enemies live there, in the ruins. They make war on us—and the Star Giants watch. It amuses them."

"These Tunnel City men—they're men, like us? I mean, not giants?"

"They're like us, all right. That's why they fight us. The different ones don't bother."

"Different?"

"You'll find out. Stop asking questions, will you? There's food to be gathered." Jorn turned to a corn-haired young villager nearby. "Show Harkins where he's going to stay—and then put him to work in the grain field."

A confused swirl of thoughts cascaded through Harkins' mind as the young man led him away. Slowly, the jigsaw was fitting together.

The villagers spoke a sort of English, which spiked Harkins' theory that he had somehow been cast backward in time. The alternative, hard as it was to accept, was plain: he was in the future, in a strangely altered world.

The Star Giants—who were they? Jorn had said they watched while the contending villages fought. It amused them, he said. That argued that the giants were the dominant forces in this world. Were they humans? Invaders from elsewhere? Those questions would have to wait for answers. Jorn either didn't know them; or didn't want Harkins to know.

The robot in the forest—unexplained. The Star Giant had shown it a healthy respect, though.

The tribe here—Jorn was in command, and everyone appeared to respect his authority. A fairly conventional primitive arrangement, Harkins thought. It implied an almost total breakdown of civilization some time in the past. The pieces were fitting together, though there were gaps.

The Tunnel City, home of the hated enemy. "One of the Old Places," Jorn had said. The enemies lived in the ruins. That was clear enough. But what of these "different ones"?

He shook his head. It was a strange and confusing world, and possibly the fewer questions he asked the safer he would be.

"Here's our place," the villager said. He pointed to a long hut, low and broad. "The single men stay here. Take any bed that has no clothing on it."

"Thanks," said Harkins. He stooped to enter. The

10

interior of the hut was crude and bare, with straw pallets scattered at random here and there inside. He selected one that looked fairly clean and dropped his jacket on it. "This is mine," he said.

The other nodded. "Now to the grain fields." He pointed to a clearing behind the village.

Harkins spent the rest of that afternoon working in the fields, deliberately using as much energy as he could and trying not to think. By the time night approached, he was thoroughly exhausted. The men returned to the village, where the women served a plain but nourishing community supper.

The simple life, Harkins thought. Farming and gathering food and occasional intertribal conflicts. It was hardly a lofty position these remote descendants of his had reached, he observed wryly. And something was wrong with the picture. The breakdown must have occured fairly recently, for them to be still sunk this low in cultural pattern—but the thickness of the forestation implied many centuries had gone by since this area had been heavily populated. There was a hole in his logical construct here, Harkins realized, and he was unable to find it.

Night came. The moon was full, and he stared at its pockmarked face longingly, feeling a strong homesickness for the crowded, busy world he had been taken from. He looked at the tribesmen sprawled on the ground, their bellies full, their bodies tired. Someone was singing a tuneless, unmelodic song. Loud snoring came from behind him. Jorn stood tensely outlined against the brightness of the moon, staring out toward the forest as if expecting a momentary invasion. From far away came the thumping sound of a robot crashing its way through the trees, or possibly a Star Giant bound on some unknown errand.

Suddenly Jorn turned. "Time for sleep," he snapped, "into your huts."

He moved around, kicking the dozers, shoving the women away from the fire. *He's the boss, all right,* Harkins thought. He studied Jorn's whipcord muscles appreciatively, and decided he'd do his best to avoid crossing the big man, for the duration of his stay in the village.

Later, Harkins lay on his rough bed, trying to sleep. It was impossible. The bright moonlight streamed in the open door of the hut, and in any event he was too tense for sleep to come. He craned his neck, looking around. The six men with whom he shared the hut were sound asleep, reaping the reward of their hard day's toil. They had security, he thought—the security of ignorance. He, Harkins, had too much of the civilized man's perceptivity. The night-noises from outside disturbed him, the muffled booms from the forest woke strange and deeply buried terrors in him. This was no world for nervous men.

He closed his eyes and lay back again. The image of the Star Giant floated before him, first the Star Giant-as-tree, then the complete entity, finally just the oddly benign, melancholy face. He pictured the Star Giants gathered together, wherever they lived, moving with massive grace and bowing elegantly to each other in a fantastic minuet. He wondered if the one who had found him today had been aware he carried an intelligent being, or if he had been thought of as some two-legged forest creature too small to regard seriously.

The image of the robot haunted him then—the domeheaded, indomitable creature pursuing some incomprehensible design, driving relentlessly through the forest toward a hidden goal. Weaving in and out of his thoughts was the screaming of the toothed birds, and the booming thunder of the forest. *A world I never made,* he thought tiredly, and tried to force sleep to take him.

Suddenly, something brushed his arm lightly. He sat up in an instant and narrowed his eyes to see.

"Don't make any noise," a soft voice said.

Katha.

She was crouched over his pallet, looking intently down at him. He wondered how long she had been there. Her free-flowing hair streamed down over her shoulders, and her nostrils flickered expectantly as Harkins moved toward her.

"What are you doing here?"

"Come outside," she whispered. "We don't want to wake *them*."

Harkins allowed her to lead him outside. Moonlight illuminated the scene clearly. The sleeping village was utterly quiet, and the eerie jungle sounds could be heard with ease.

"Jorn is with Nella tonight," Katha said bitterly. "I am usually Jorn's woman—but tonight he ignored me."

Harkins frowned. Tired as he was, he could see what the situation was immediately, and he didn't like it at all. Katha was going to use him as a way of expressing her jealousy to Jorn.

She moved closer to him and pressed her warm body against his. Involuntarily, he accepted the embrace—and then stepped back. Regardless of Katha's motives, Jorn would probably kill him on the spot if he woke and found him with her. The girl was a magnificent animal, he thought regretfully, and perhaps some other time, some other place—

But not here, not now. Harkins was dependent on

Jorn's mercies, and it was important to remain in his good graces. Gently, he pushed Katha back.

"No," he said. "You belong to Jorn."

Her nostrils flared. "I belong to no one!" she whispered harshly. She came toward him again. There was the sound of someone stirring in a nearby hut.

"Go back to sleep," Harkins said anxiously. "If Jorn finds us, he'll kill us both."

"Jorn is busy with that child Nella—but he would not kill me anyway. Are you afraid of Jorn, stranger?"

"No," Harkins lied. "I—"

"You talk like a coward!" Again, she seized him, and this time he shoved her away roughly. She spat angrily at him and slapped him in fury. Then she cupped her hand and cried, *"Help!"*

At her outcry, Harkins dodged past her and attempted to re-enter his hut, but he was much too late. The whole village seemed to be awake in an instant, and before he was fully aware of what had happened he felt a firm pressure on the back of his neck.

"The rest of you go back to bed." It was Jorn's voice, loud and commanding, and in a moment the square was empty again—except for Katha, Harkins, and Jorn. The big man held Harkins by the neck with one hand and a squirming, struggling Katha with the other.

"He attacked me!" Katha accused.

"It's a lie!"

"Quiet, both of you!" Jorn's voice snapped like a whip. He let go of Katha and threw her to the ground, where she remained, kneeling subserviently. His grip on Harkins tightened.

"What happened?" Jorn demanded.

"Let her tell it," Harkins replied.

"Her word is meaningless. I want the truth."

"He came to my hut and attacked me," Katha said. "It was because he knew you were busy with Nella—"

Jorn silenced her with a kick. "She came to you, did she not?"

Harkins nodded. "Yes."

"I thought so. I expected it. This has happened before." He released Harkins, and gestured for Katha to take her feet. "You will have to leave here," Jorn said. "Katha is mine."

"But—"

"It is not your fault," Jorn said. "But you must leave here. She will not rest until she has you. Go now—and if you return, I will have to kill you."

Harkins felt numb at Jorn's words. The last thing he would have wanted to happen was to be thrust out of the one haven he had found so far in this strange and unfriendly world. He looked at Katha, who was glaring at him in bitter hatred, her breasts rising and falling rapidly in rage. He began to feel rage himself at the unfairness of the situation.

He watched as Jorn turned to Katha. "Your punishment will come later. You will pay for this, Katha."

She bowed her head, then looked up. With astonishment, Harkins saw that she was looking at Jorn with unmistakable love reflected in her eyes.

Jorn gestured toward the forest. "Go."

"Right now?"

"Now," Jorn said. "You must be gone by morning. I should not have allowed you to stay at all."

CHAPTER III

WHATEVER personal deity was looking out for him was doing a notably bad job, Harkins thought, as he stood at the edge of the forest. It was sadistic to bring him into contact with a civilization, of sorts, and then almost immediately thrust him back into the uncertainty of the forest.

It was near dawn. He had spent most of the night circling the borders of the clearing, postponing the moment when he would have to enter the forest again. He withdrew to the edge of the clearing and waited there. For a while, there had been the sound of repeated snapping, as of a whip descending, coming from Jorn's hut. Then, there had been silence. Harkins wondered whether Katha's punishment had not, perhaps, been followed by a reward.

Jorn had been right to cast him out, Harkins admitted. In a tribal set-up of that sort, the leader's dominance had to be maintained—and any possible competitor, even such an unwilling one as Harkins, had to be expelled. Now that Harkins considered the matter, he realized that Jorn had been surprisingly lenient not to kill him on the spot.

Only—facing this strange, wild world alone would be no joyride.

As the first faint rays of dawn began to break on the horizon, Harkins entered the forest. Almost immediately, the air changed, grew cooler and damper. The thick curtain of vegetation that roofed in the forest kept the sunlight out. Harkins moved warily, following the trampled path the Star Giant had left.

Somewhere not too far from here would be the Tunnel City. It would have to be reasonably close: in a non-mechanized society such as this, it would be impossible to carry out warfare over any great distance. And the Tunnel City, whatever it was, was inhabited. He hoped he would be able to locate it before he encountered any trouble in the forest. As an outcast from Jorn's group, he could probably gain refuge there.

Suddenly there was the sound of crashing timber up ahead. He flattened himself against a lichen-covered rock and peered into the distance.

Above the trees, the red-brown head of a Star Giant on his way through the forest was visible. Harkins considered momentarily going toward the giant, but then changed his mind and struck off along a back path. The Star Giants had let him live once, but there was no predicting their actions. There was little choice in the matter anyway; the Star Giant was rapidly moving on, covering forty feet at a stride.

Harkins watched the huge being until it was out of sight, and then continued to walk. Perhaps, he thought, the path might lead to the Tunnel City. Perhaps not. At this point, he had very little to lose no matter which direction he took.

But he was wrong. The other path might have been safe; this one was barred by a howling nightmare.

It was facing him squarely, its six legs braced

17

between two thin trees. The creature had a pair of snapping mouths—one on each flattened, sharp-snouted head. Razor-like teeth glistened in the dim light. Harkins froze, unable either to turn and run or to dash forward on the offensive. The creature's howling rose to a frantic pitch that served as wild counterpoint for the dull booming of the forest.

The thing began to advance. Harkins felt sweat trickle down his body. The animal, white-furred, was the size of a large wolf, and looked hungry. Harkins retreated, feeling his way cautiously at each step, while the animal gathered itself to leap.

Without conscious forethought Harkins extended a hand toward a dead tree behind him and yanked down on a limb. It broke off, showering him with flaky bark. As the monster sprang, he brought the crude club around in baseball-bat fashion.

It crashed into the gaping mouth of the animal's nearest head, and teeth splintered against dry wood. Quickly Harkins ran forward and jammed the tree-limb between the jaws of the other head, immobilizing them. The animal clawed at Harkins, but its upper arms were too short.

Stalemate. Harkins held the animal at arm's length. It raged and spat impotently, unable to reach him. He did not dare let go, but his strength couldn't hold out indefinitely, he knew.

Slowly, clawing futilely, the animal forced him backward. Harkins felt the muscles of his upper arms quivering from the strain; he pushed backward, and the animal howled in pain. The other head gnashed its ruined teeth savagely.

Overhead, strange bird-cries resounded, and once Harkins glanced upward to see a row of placid, bright-wattled birds waiting impassively on a tree-limb. Their mouths glittered toothily, and they were like no birds he had ever seen before, but he knew instinctively what function they served in the forest. They were vultures, ready to go to work as soon as the stalemate broke.

And it was going to break soon. Harkins would be unable to hold the maddened animal off for long. His fingers were trembling, and soon the log would slip from his grasp. And then—

A flashing metallic hand reached down from somewhere above, and abruptly the pressure relaxed. To his astonishment, Harkins watched the hand draw the animal upward.

He followed it with his eyes. A robot stood over them, faceless, inhuman, contemplating the fierce beast it held in its metal grip. Harkins blinked. He had become so involved in the struggle that he had not heard the robot's approach.

The robot seized the animal by each of its throats, and *tore*. Casually, it flipped the still-living body into the shrubbery, where it thrashed for a moment and subsided—and then the robot continued through the forest, while the vultures from the tree-limb swooped down upon their prize.

Harkins sank down on a decaying stump and sucked in his breath. His overtensed arms shook violently and uncontrollably.

It was as if the robot had been sent there for the mission of destroying the carnivore—and, mission completed, had returned to its base, having no further interest in Harkins' doings.

I'm just a pawn, he thought suddenly. The realization hit him solidly, and he slumped in weariness.

19

That was the answer, of course: pawn. He was being manipulated. He had been shunted out of his own era, thrown in and out of Jorn's village, put in and out of deadly peril. It was a disquieting thought, and one that robbed him of his strength for some minutes. He knew his limitations, but he had liked to think of himself as master of his fate. He wasn't, now.

All right—where do I go from here?

No answer came. Deciding that his manipulator was busy somewhere else on the chessboard at the moment, he pulled himself to his feet and slowly began to move deeper into the forest.

He walked warily this time, keeping an eye out for wildlife. There might not be any robots' hands to rescue him, the next time.

The forest seemed calm again. Harkins walked step by step, moving further and further into the heart of the woods, leaving Jorn's village far behind. It was getting toward afternoon, and he was starting to tire.

He reached a bubbling spring and dropped gratefully by its side. The water looked fresh and clear; he dipped a hand in, feeling the refreshing coolness, and wet his fingers. Drawing the hand out, he touched it experimentally to his lips. The water tasted pure, but he wrinkled his forehead in doubt.

"Go ahead and drink," a dry voice said suddenly. "The water's perfectly good."

Harkins sprang up instantly. "Who said that?"

"I did."

He looked around. "I don't see anybody. Where are you?"

"Up here on the rock," the voice said. "Over here, silly."

20

Harkins turned in the direction of the voice—and saw the speaker. "Who—what are you?"

"Men call me the Watcher," came the calm reply. The Watcher was mounted on the huge rock through whose cleft base the stream flowed. Harkins saw a man, or something like a man, with gray-green, rugose skin, pale, sightless eyes, and tiny, dangling boneless arms. Its mouth was wide and grotesque, contorted into something possibly intended to be a grin.

Harkins took a step backward in awe and surprise.

"I'm not pretty," the Watcher said. "But you don't have to run. I won't hurt you. Go on—drink your fill, and then we can talk."

"No," Harkins said uneasily. "Who are you, anyway? What are you doing here?"

The thick lips writhed in a terrifying smirk. "What am *I* doing here? I have been here for two thousand years and more, now. I might ask what *you* are doing here."

"I—don't know," Harkins said.

"I know you don't know," the Watcher said mockingly. He emitted an uproarious chuckle, and his soft, pale belly jiggled obscenely. "Of course you don't know! How could you be expected to know?"

"I don't like riddles," Harkins said, feeling angry and sensing the strange unreality of the conversation. "What are you?"

"I was a man, once." Suddenly the mocking tone was gone. "My parents were human. I—am not."

"Parents?"

"Thousands of years ago. In the days before the War. In the days before the Star Giants came." The wide mouth drooped sadly. "In the world that once

21

was—the world you were drawn from, poor mystified thing."

"Just what do you know about me?" Harkins demanded.

"Too much," said the Watcher wearily. "Take your drink first, and then I'll explain."

Harkins' throat felt as if it had been sandpapered. He knelt and let the cool brook water enter. Finally, he rose. The Watcher had not moved; he remained seated on the rock, his tiny, useless arms folded in bizarre parody of a human gesture.

"Sit down," the Watcher said. "I have a story two thousand years long to tell."

Harkins took a seat on a stone and leaned against a tree trunk. The Watcher began to speak.

The story began in Harkins' own time, or shortly afterward. The Watcher traced the history of the civilization that had developed in the early centuries of the Third Millennium, told of the rise of the underground cities and the people who had built the robots that still roved the forest.

War had come—destroying that society completely, save for a few bands of survivors. Some of the cities had survived too, but the minds that had guided the robot brains were gone, and the robots continued to function in the duties last assigned. The underground cities had become taboo places, though savage bands lived above them, never venturing beneath the surface.

Down below, in the tunnels of the dead ones, the mutant descendants of the city-builders lived. The Different Ones, those of whom Jorn had spoken. Most of them lived in the cities; a few others in the forests.

"I am one of those," said the Watcher. "I have not moved from this spot since the year the Star Giants came."

"The Star Giants," Harkins said. "Who are they?"

The flabby shoulders shrugged. "They came from the stars, long after we had destroyed ourselves. They live here, watching the survivors with great curiousity. They toy with the tribes, set them in conflict with each other, and study the results with deep interest. For some reason they don't bother me. They seem never to pass this way in the forest."

"And the robots?"

"They'll continue as they are till the end of time. Nothing can destroy them, nothing can swerve them from their activity—and nothing can command them."

Harkins leaned forward intently. The Watcher had given him all the answers he needed but one.

"Why am *I* here?" he asked.

"You?" The mutant laughed coldly. "You're the random factor. It would ruin the game to tell you too many answers. But I'll grant you this much information: *You can go home if you get control of the robots.*"

"What? How?"

"Find that out for yourself," the Watcher said. "I'll keep a close lookout for you, blind as I am, but I won't help you more than I have."

Harkins smiled and said, "What if I force you to tell me?"

"How could you possibly do that?" Again the wide lips contorted unpleasantly. "How could you ever force me to do anything I didn't want to do?"

"Like this," Harkins said, in sudden rage. He pried out of the earth the stone he was sitting on and hoisted it above his head.

No.

It was a command, unvoiced. The stone tumbled from Harkins' nerveless hands and thudded to the ground. Harkins stared at his numbed fingers.

"You learn slowly," the Watcher said. "I am blind, but that doesn't mean I don't see—or react. I repeat: how could you force me to do anything?"

"I—can't," Harkins said hesitantly.

"Good. Admission of weakness is the first step toward strength. Understand that I brought you to me deliberately, that at no time during this interview have you operated under your own free will, and that I'm perfectly capable of determining your future actions if I see fit. I don't, however, care that greatly to interfere."

"*You're* the chess player, then!" Harkins said accusingly.

"Only one of them," the mutant said. "And the least important of them." He unfolded his pitiful arms. "I brought you to me for no other reason than diversion—and now you tire me. It is time for you to leave."

"Where do I go?"

"The nerve-center of the situation is in Tunnel City," the Watcher said. "You must pass through there on your way home. Leave me."

Without waiting for a second command, Harkins rose and began to walk away. After ten steps, he glanced back. The Watcher's arms were folded once across his chest again.

"Keep going," the mutant said. "You've served your purpose."

Harkins nodded and started walking again. *I'm still a pawn,* he thought bitterly. *But—whose pawn am I?*

CHAPTER IV

AFTER HE put a considerable distance between himself and the Watcher, Harkins paused by the side of a
ponderous grainy-barked tree and tried to assimilate
the new facts.

A game was being played out between forces too
great for his comprehension. He had been drawn into
it for reasons unknown, and—unless the Watcher
had lied—the way out for him lay through Tunnel
City.

He had no idea where that city was, nor did he
know what he was supposed to find there. *You can go
home if you get control of the robots,* the Watcher
had said. And the strange mutant had implied that
Tunnel City was the control-center of the robots. But
he had also said that nothing could command the
robots!

Harkins smiled. There must be a way for him to get
there. The time had come for him to do some manipu-
lation of his own. He had been a puppet long enough;
now he would pull a few strings.

He looked up. Late afternoon shadows were starting to fall, and the sky was darkening. He would have
to move quickly if he wanted to get there by nightfall.
Rapidly, he began to retrace his steps through the

forest, following the beaten path back toward Jorn's village. He traveled quickly, half walking, half running. Now and then he saw the bald head of a Star Giant looming up above a faroff treetop, but the aliens paid no attention to him. Once, he heard the harsh sound of a robot driving through the underbrush.

Strange forces were at play here. The Star Giants—who were they? What did they want on Earth—and what part did they take in the drama now unfolding? They seemed remote, detached, as totally unconcerned with the pattern of events as the mindless robots that moved through the forest. Yet Harkins knew that that was untrue.

The robots interested him philosophically. They represented Force—unstoppable, uncontrollable Force, tied to some pre-set and long-forgotten pattern of activity. Why had the robot saved him from the carnivore? Was that part of the network of happenings, he wondered, or did the chess game take precedence over even the robot activity-pattern?

There was the interesting personal problem of the relationship between Jorn and Katha, too; it was a problem he would be facing again soon. Katha loved Jorn, obviously—and, with savage ambivalence, hated him as well. Harkins wondered just where he would fit into the situation when he returned to Jorn's village. Jorn and Katha were many-sided, unpredictable people; and he depended on their whims for the success of his plan.

Wheels within wheels, he thought wryly. Pawns in one game dictate the moves in a smaller one. He stepped up his pace; night was approaching rapidly. The forest grew cold.

The village became visible at last, a huddled gray clump half-seen through the heavy fronds of the forest. Harkins slowed to a walk as he drew near.

It was still early; the villagers had not yet eaten their community supper. Harkins paused at the edge of the forest, standing by a deadly-looking tree whose leaves were footlong spikes of golden horn, and wondered what was the safest way of approaching the village.

Suddenly, a twig crackled behind him. He turned.

"I thought I told you never to come back here, Harkins. What are you doing here, now?"

"I came back to talk to you, Jorn."

The big man was wearing only a loincloth, and his long-limbed body, covered by a thick black mat of hair, looked poised for combat. A muscle twitched uncontrollably in Jorn's cheek.

"What do you want to talk about?"

"The Tunnel City," Harkins said.

"I don't want to hear about it," Jorn snapped. "I said I'd kill you if you cme back here, and I meant it. I don't want you playing with Katha."

"I wasn't playing with Katha. She threw herself on me."

"Same thing," Jorn said. "In the eyes of the tribe, I'm being betrayed. I can't have that, Harkins." The rumbling voice sounded almost desperate. Harkins saw suddenly how close to insanity the power-drive was, when it cropped out as nakedly as in this pure dictatorship.

"Would you really *need* Katha," Harkins asked, "if I made you lord of the world?"

"What do you mean by that?" Jorn sounded suspicious, but interested despite himself.

"I spoke to the Watcher." Harkins said. The name provoked an immediate reaction. Jorn paled, licked his lips nervously, darted his eyes from side to side.

"You—spoke to the Watcher?"

Harkins nodded. "He told me how to win Tunnel City. You can conquer the world, Jorn, if you listen to me!"

"Explain." It was a flat command.

"You know what's underneath Tunnel City?"

Again Jorn paled. "Yes." he said hoarsely. "We don't go there. It's bad."

"I can go there. I'm not afraid of it." Harkins grinned triumphantly. "Jorn, I can go down there and make the robots work for me. With them on our side, we can conquer the world. We—"

Instantly, he saw he had made a mistake. One word had done it—*we*. Jorn had stiffened, and was beginning to arch his back with deadly intent.

"We won't do anything of the kind," Jorn said coldly.

Harkins tried to cover. "I mean—I'll make the robots work and you can control them! You'll be the leader; I'll just—"

"Who are you fooling, Harkins? You'll try to take power away from me, once you have the robots. Don't deny it."

"I'm *not* denying it. Dammit, wouldn't you rather rule half the world than *all* of this little mudhole here?"

It was another mistake—and a worse one than the last. This mistake was fatal, because it struck Jorn precisely where he was most brittle.

"*I'll kill you!*" Jorn screamed, and charged forward.

Harkins stepped back and readied himself for the big man's frenzied assault. Jorn struck him squarely, knocked him backward, and leaped on him.

Harkins felt powerful hands reaching for his throat. Desperately, he seized Jorn's wrists and pulled them away. The big man moved with almost cat-like grace, rolling over and over with Harkins while the birds squalled in delight overhead.

Harkins felt fists pummeling his stomach. Jorn was sitting astride him now, unable to get at this throat for the fatal throttling but determined to do all the damage he could nonetheless. Through a haze of pain, Harkins managed to wriggle out from under Jorn and get to his feet, breathing hard. A trickle of blood wound saltily over his tongue and out the corner of his mouth.

Jorn backed off. The adversaries faced each other. Harkins felt cold, almost icy; this would have to be a battle to the death, and somehow he suspected there would be no interference by robots or Star Giants this time.

He had blundered seriously in his approach. He needed Jorn's guidance in order to reach the Tunnel City—but by implying a sharing of power, he had scraped raw nerves in the tribal leader. And, thought Harkins, his final remark had been sheer stupidity; a logical man would prefer half an empire to an entire squiredom, but Jorn was not logical.

"Come on," Jorn said beckoning with a powerful fist. "Come close where I can reach you."

Harkins considered flight, then abandoned the idea. It was getting dark; besides, Jorn could probably outrun him.

No; he would have to stand and face it.

Jorn stepped forward, holding his huge hands out invitingly. As he lunged, Harkins sidestepped and clubbed down hard on Jorn's neck. The big man wavered at the rabbit-punch, but did not fall. Harkins followed up his advantage by pounding three quick and ineffectual blows to Jorn's sides, and then the big man recovered.

He seized Harkins by one arm and drew him close. *Sorry,* Harkins thought unregretfully, and brought up one knee. Jorn let go and doubled up.

Harkins was on him in an instant—but, to his surprise, he found that Jorn was still in full command of himself despite the kneeing. The big man put his head down and butted. Harkins fell over backward, gasping for air, clawing at the sky. It had been like being hit in the stomach by a battering ram—and for a dizzy second Harkins felt that he was about to drown on dry land.

Jorn was moving in for the kill now. Once he reached the throat, it would be all over. Harkins watched helplessly as the big hands lowered. Jorn leaned forward.

Suddenly, Harkins kicked upward, and with what little strength he had left, he *pushed*. Hard. Jorn, taken unawares, lost his balance, toppled backward—

And to Harkins' horror fell against the spine-tree at the edge of the little clearing.

Jorn screamed—just once—as the foot-long spike of bone slipped between his vertebrae. He struggled fitfully for a fraction of an instant, then subsided and stared bitterly and perplexedly at Harkins until his eyes closed. A few drops of blood mingled with the matted hair on Jorn's chest. The tip of the spike was barely visible, a mere eighth of an inch protruding near Jorn's left breast.

It had obviously penetrated his heart.

Harkins looked uncomprehendingly at the impaled man for a full thirty seconds, not yet realizing that the contest was over and he had won. He had fully expected to lose, fully expected this to be his last hour—and, instead, Jorn lay dead. It had happened too quickly.

A lurking shadow dropped over the scene. Harkins glanced up. A Star Giant stood about a hundred feet away, hipdeep in low-lying shrubs, staring far out into the distance. Harkins wondered if the huge alien had witnessed the combat.

The adrenalin was draining out of his system now. Calming, he tried to evaluate the situation as it now stood. With Jorn dead, the next move would be to establish control over the tribe himself. And that—

"Jorn!" a feminine voice cried. "Jorn, are you in there? We're waiting to eat."

Harkins turned. "Hello, Katha."

She stared stonily past him. "Where's Jorn?" she asked. "What are you doing back here?"

"Jorn's over there," Harkins said cruelly, and stepped aside to let her see.

The look in her eyes was frightening. She turned from Jorn's body to Harkins and said, "Did you do this?"

"He attacked me. He was out of his mind."

"You killed him," she said dully. "You killed Jorn."

"Yes," Harkins said.

The girl's jaw tightened, and she spat contemptuously. Without further warning, she sprang.

It was like the leap of a tigress. Harkins, still exhausted from his encounter with Jorn, was not prepared for the fury of her onslaught, and he was forced to throw his hands up wildly to keep her fingernails from his eyes. She threw him to the ground, locked her thighs around his waist tightly, and punched, bit, and scratched.

After nearly a minute of this, Harkins managed to grab her wrists. *She's more dangerous than Jorn,* he thought, as he bent her arms backward and slowly forced her to release her leglock. He drew her to her feet and held her opposite him. Her jaws were working convulsively.

"You killed him," she repeated. "I'll kill you now."

Harkins released her arms and she sprang away, shaking her long hair, flexing her bare legs. Her breasts, covered casually by two strips of cloth, rose and fell rapidly. He watched in astonishment as she went into a savage war-dance, bending and posturing, circling around him. It was a ritual of revenge, he thought. The tigress was avenging her mate against the outsider.

Suddenly she broke from her dance and ran to the tree on which Jorn lay impaled. She broke loose one of the golden spikes and, holding it knifewise, advanced once again toward Harkins.

He glanced around, found a fallen log, and brandished it. She moved in, knife held high, while Harkins waited for her to come within reach.

Her magnificent legs bowed and carried her through the air. Harkins moved intuitively, throwing up his left arm to ward off the blow and bringing his right, holding the club, around in a crossblow. The log crashed into the underside of her wrist; she uttered an involuntary grunt of pain and dropped the spike. Harkins kicked it to one side and grabbed her.

He hugged her against him, pinioning her arms against her sides. She kicked her legs in frustration until, seeing she could do no harm, she subsided.

"Now you have me, Lloyd Harkins—until you let go."

"Don't worry, tigress—I'll hold you here until there's no fight left in you."

"That will be forever!"

"So be it," Harkins said. He leaned closer to her ear. "You're very lovely when you're blazing mad, you know."

"When I came to you, you refused me, coward. Will you now insult me before Jorn's dead body?"

"Jorn deserved what he got," Harkins said. "I offered him an empire—and he refused me. He couldn't bear the thought of sharing his power with anyone."

The girl remained silent for a moment. Finally she said, in an altered voice, "Yes—Jorn was like that."

"It was kill or be killed," Harkins said. "Jorn was a madman. I had to—"

"Don't talk about it!" she snapped. Then: "What of this empire?" Greedy curiosity seemed to replace anger.

"Something the Watcher told me."

Katha reacted as Jorn had; fear crossed her face, and she turned her head to one side to avoid Harkins' eyes. "The Watcher showed me where the secret of power lies," he said. "I told Jorn—"

"*Where?*"

"Tunnel City," he said. "If I could go there at the head of an army, I could take control of the robots. With them on our side, we would conquer the world." *If* the Watcher was telling the truth, he added silently. And *if* he could find the way to control the robots.

"The Star Giants would never let you," Katha said.

"I don't understand." He relaxed the pressure on the girl's arms slightly, and she tensed. It was like sitting on a bolt of lightning, he thought.

"The Star Giants keep us in small groups," she said. "Whenever there is danger of our forming an army or a city, they break it up. Somehow they always know. So you would never be allowed to conquer the world. They would not permit it."

"So this is their laboratory, then?" he said, as a bit more of the picture became clear.

"What?"

"I mean—the Star Giants watch and study you. They keep the social groups down to manageable size—seventy, eighty, no more. They experiment in psychology."

An image filtered through his mind—a world in a test tube, held by a wise-faced, deeply curious Star Giant who was unable to regard anything so small as a man as an intelligent being. Men were serving as so many fruitflies for the Star Giants—who, without any evil motives, out of sheer scientific interest, were deliberately preventing human civilization from re-forming. A pulse of anger started to beat in him.

"I don't follow you," she said. "They watch us only because they like to?"

How to explain the concept of lab research to a savage? he wondered. "Yes," he said. "They watch you."

She frowned. "But you can control the robots? Harkins, perhaps the Star Giants will not be able to stop the robots. Perhaps—"

He didn't need a further suggestion. "You're right! If I can gain control of the robots, I can smash the Star Giants—drive them back to where they came from!"

Was it true? He didn't know—but it was worth a try. In sudden excitement he leaped away, freeing the girl.

She hadn't forgotten revenge. Instantly she was upon him, knocking him to the ground. He rolled over, but she clung to him. At that moment, a deep shadow swept down over both of them.

"Look up there," Harkins said in a hushed voice.

They stared upward together. A Star Giant was standing above them, his treelike legs straddling them, peering down with an expression of grave concern on his massive, sculpture-like face.

"He's watching us," she said.

"Now do you understand? He's *observing*—trying to learn what kind of creatures these little animals on the forest floor may be." He wondered briefly if this entire three-cornered scene—Harkins versus Jorn, then Harkins versus Katha—had been arranged merely for the edification of the monstrous creature standing above them. A new image crossed his mind—himself and Katha in a vast laboratory, struggling with each other within the confines of a chemical retort held by a quizzical Star Giant. His flesh felt cold.

Katha turned from the Star Giant to Harkins. "I hate them," she said. "We will kill them together." With the fickleness of a savage, she had forgotten all about her anger.

"No more fighting?"

She grinned, flashing bright white teeth, and relaxed her grip on Harkins. "Truce," she said.

He pulled her back close to him, and put his mouth to hers wondering if the Star Giant was still watching.

She giggled childishly and bit deep into Harkins' lower lip. "That was for Jorn," she said, her voice a playful purr. "Now the score is even."

She pressed tightly against him, and kissed the blood away.

CHAPTER V

HE WAS greeted by suspicious stares and awkward silences when he returned to the village.

"Jorn is dead," Katha announced. "Harkins and Jorn met in combat at the edge of the forest."

"And now Jorn is beneath the ground," cackled the ugly woman named Elsa. "I saw it coming, brothers. You can't deny that I warned him."

"Harkins is our leader now," Katha said firmly. "And I am his woman."

The sleepy-eyed villager who had voted for Harkins' life once said, "Who has elected him?"

"*I* have, Dujar," Harkins said. He doubled his fists. In a society such as this, you had to back up your chips at all times. "Who objects?"

Dujar looked helplessly at the witch-woman Elsa. "Is it good?"

She shrugged. "Yes and no. Choose as you see fit."

The sleepy-eyed man frowned worriedly, but said nothing. Harkins glanced from one face to the next. "Is there anyone who objects to my leading this tribe?"

"We don't even know who you are!" a thick-faced man said. "How do we know you're not a spy from the Tunnel City people? Elsa, is he?"

"I thought so once," the squat woman said. "I'm not so sure now."

Harkins smiled. "We'll see if I am or not. Tomorrow we march. Prepare for war—against the Tunnel City people."

"War? But—"

"War," Harkins said. It was a flat statement, a command. "Elsa, can you make maps?"

Elsa nodded sullenly.

"Good. Come to my hut now, and I'll tell you what I need."

The witch-woman grinned wickedly. "What say you, Katha—will you trust me with your man alone?"

"No—I want Katha there too," Harkins said quickly.

Disappointment was evident on Elsa's sallow face; Katha's eyes had flickered with momentary anger at Elsa's remark, though she had not replied. Harkins frowned. Another complex relationship seemed to be developing, and a dangerous one. He needed Elsa's support; she was a potent figure in the tribe. But he didn't know whether or not he could depend on her for continuing aid.

He stared down at the map scratched in the smooth dirt floor of his hut. "This is the situation, then?"

He glanced from Elsa to Katha. Both women nodded.

Gesturing with his toe, Harkins said, "We are here, and the Tunnel City is two days' march to the east. Right?"

"It is as I have said," Elsa replied.

"And the Star Giants live somewhere out here," Harkins said, pointing to a vaguely-bounded area somewhere on the far side of the great forest.

"Why do you want to know the home of the Star Giants?" Elsa asked. "You struck down Jorn—but that doesn't grant you a giant's strength, Harkins."

"Quiet, Elsa." The woman's needling was starting to irritate him. And Katha was showing signs of jealousy, which disturbed him. She was fiercely possessive, but just as fiercely inclined to hate as to love, and Harkins could easily visualize a situation in which both these women were turned against him. He repressed a shudder and returned his attention to the map.

"Elsa, tonight you'll lead the tribe in prayers for the success of our campaign. And tomorrow, the men will leave for Tunnel City."

"And which of us accompanies you?" Katha asked coldly.

"You," Harkins said. Before Elsa could reply, he added, "Elsa, you'll be needed here, to cast defensive spells over the village while the warriors are gone."

She chuckled hollowly. "A clever assignment, Harkins. Very well. I accept the task." She looked at him, eyes glinting craftily. "Tell me something, though."

"What is it?"

"*Why* are you attacking the Tunnel City people just now? What do you stand to gain by a needless war?"

"I stand to gain a world, Elsa," Harkins said quietly, and would say no more.

That night, ritual drums sounded at the edge of the forest, and strange incantations were pronounced. Harkins watched, fascinated at the curious mixture of barbarism and sophistication.

They left the following morning, twenty-three men led by Harkins and Katha. It represented the entire fighting strength of the tribe, minus a couple of disgruntled oldsters who were left behind on the pretext that the village needed a defensive force.

The journey to the Tunnel City was a slow and halting one. A tall warrior named Frugo was appointed to guide, at Katha's suggestion; he kept them skirting the edge of the forest until well into midafternoon, when they were forced to strike off through the jungle.

Katha marched proudly at Harkins' side, as if Jorn had never existed. And, perhaps, in this historyless world, he *had* never existed, now that he was dead.

The war party sustained itself as it went. Two of the men were experts with the throwing-stick, and brought down an ample supply of birds for the evening meal; another gathered basketsful of a curious golden-green fruit. While the birds were being cleaned and cooked, Harkins picked one up and examined it, opening its jaws to peer at the teeth.

It was an interesting mutation—a recession to a characteristic lost thousands of years earlier. He studied the fierce-looking bird for a moment or two, then tossed it back on the heap.

"Never seen a bird before?" Katha asked.

"Not that kind," Harkins said. He turned away and walked toward the fire, where three were being roasted over a greenwood fire. A sound of crashing trees was audible far in the distance.

"Star Giant?" he asked.

"Robot, probably," Katha said. "They make more noise. Star Giants look where they're going.

41

The robots just bull straight ahead.''

Harkins nodded. "That's what I hope they'll do when they're working for us. Straight on through the Star Giants.''

A twisted-looking brown wingless bird with a bulging breast came running along the forest path, squawking and flapping its vestigial stumps. It ran straight into the little camp; then, seeing where it was, it turned and tried to run away. It was too late, though; a grinning warrior caught it by the throat and pulled the protesting bird toward the fire.

"They keep going straight too,'' Katha said. "Straight into the fire.''

"I think we'll manage,'' Harkins said. He wished he were as sure as he sounded.

The Tunnel City sprawled over some ten square miles of land, bordered on all sides by the ever-approaching forest. Harkins and his men stood on a cliff looking down at the ruined city.

The crumbling buildings were old—ancient, even—but from the style of their architecture Harkins saw that they had been built after his time. What might once have been airy needles of chrome and concrete now were blackened hulks slowly vanishing beneath the onslaught of the jungle.

Harkins turned to Katha. "How many people live here?''

"About a hundred. They live in the big building down there,'' she said, pointing to a truncated spire.

"And the entrance to the tunnels themselves?''

She shuddered faintly. "In the center of the city. No one goes there.''

"I know that,'' Harkins said. The situation was

somewhat different from expectation. He had vis-
ualized the tribe of savages living in close proximity
to the tunnel entrance, making it necessary to conquer them before any subterranean exploration
could be done. But it seemed it would be possible to
sneak right past without the necessity of a battle.

"What's on your mind?" Katha asked.

He explained his plan. She shook her head immediately. "There'll have to be a war first. The men
won't have it any other way. They're not interested
in going into those tunnels; they just want to fight."

"All right," he said, after some thought. "Fight it
is, then. Draw up the ranks and we'll attack."

Katha cupped one hand. "Prepare to attack!"

The word traveled swiftly. Knives and clubs bris-
tled; the throwing-stick men readied themselves.
Harkins narrowly escaped smiling at the sober-
minded way this ragged band was preparing to go
about waging war with hand weapons and stones.
The smile died stillborn as he recalled that these men
fought with such crude weapons only because their
ancestors had had better ones.

He squinted toward the tangle of ruined buildings,
saw figures moving about in the city. The hated
enemy, he thought. The strangers.

"Down the hill!" he shouted.

Coolly and efficiently, the twenty-three men
peeled off down the slope and into the city. Harkins
felt ash and slag crunch underfoot as he ran with
them. The Tunnel City people were still unaware of
the approaching force; Harkins found himself hoping
they'd hear the sound in time. He wanted a battle,
not a massacre.

He turned to Katha as they ran. "As soon as the

43

battle's going well and everyone's busy, you and I are going into the tunnel.''

"No! I won't go with you!"

"There's nothing to be afraid of," Harkins said impatiently. "We—''

He stopped. The Tunnel City men had heard, now, and they came pouring out of their skyscraper home, ready to defend themselves.

The two forces came crashing together with audible impact. Harkins deliberately hung back, not out of cowardice but out of a lack of killing desire; it was more important that he survive and reach the tunnels.

One of his men drew first blood, plunging his knife into the breast of a brawny city-dweller. There was immediate retaliation; a club descended, and the killer toppled. Harkins glanced uneasily upward, wondering if the Star Giants were watching—and, if so, whether they were enjoying the spectacle.

He edged back from the milling mob and watched with satisfaction as the two forces drove at each other repeatedly. He nudged Katha. "The battle's well under way. Let's go to the tunnel."

"I'd rather fight."

"I know. But I need you down there." He grabbed her arm and whirled her around. "Are you turning coward now, Katha?"

"I—"

"There's nothing to be afraid of." He pulled her close, and kissed her roughly. "Come on, now— unless you're afraid."

She paused, fighting within herself for a moment. "All right," she agreed finally.

They backed surreptitiously away from the scene

of the conflict and ducked around a slagheap in the direction of a narrow street.

"Look out!" Katha cried suddenly.

Harkins ducked, but a knife humming through the air sliced through the flesh of his shoulder. A hot stream of blood poured down over his arm, but the wound was not serious.

He glanced around and saw who had thrown the knife. It was Dujar, the sleepy-eyed villager, who was standing on a heap of twisted metal, staring down wide-eyed at them as if unable to accept the fact that his aim had been faulty.

"Kill him!" Katha said sharply. "Kill the traitor, Harkins!"

Puzzled, Harkins turned back and started to scramble up the slagheap to reach Dujar. The villager finally snapped from his stasis and began to run, taking long-legged, awkward, rabbity strides.

Harkins bent, picked up a football-sized lump of slag, hurled it at the fleeing man's back. Dujar stumbled, fell, tried to get up. Harkins ran to him.

Dujar lifted himself from the ground and flung himself at Harkins' throat. Harkins smashed a fist into the villager's face, another into his stomach. Dujar doubled up.

Harkins seized him. "Did you throw that knife?"

No response. Harkins caught the terrified man by the throat and shook him violently. "Answer me!"

"Y-yes," Dujar finally managed to say. "I threw it."

"Why? Didn't you know who I was?"

The villager moaned piteously. "I knew who you were," he said.

"Hurry," Katha urged. "Kill the worm, and let's

get on to what we have to do."

"Just wait a minute," Harkins said. He shook Dujar again. "*Why* did you throw that knife?"

Dujar was silent for a moment, his mouth working incoherently. Then: "Elsa . . . told me to do it. She . . . said she'd poison me unless I killed you and Katha." He hung his head.

Elsa! "Remember that Katha," Harkins said. "We'll take care of her when we return to the village." The witch-woman had evidently realized she had no future with Harkins, and had decided to have him assassinated before Katha had *her* done away with.

Harkins grasped Dujar tightly. He felt pity for the man; he had been doomed either way. He glanced at Katha, saw her steely face, and knew there was only one thing he could do. Drawing his knife, he plunged it into Dujar's heart. The sleepy-eyed man glared reproachfully at Harkins for a moment, then slumped down.

It was the second time Harkins had killed. But the other had been self-defense; this had been an execution, and somehow the act made him feel filthy. He sheathed the knife, scrubbed his hands against his thighs, and stepped over the body. He knew he would have lost all authority had he let Dujar live. He would have to deal similarly with Elsa when he returned to the village.

The battle down below was still going on. "Come," Harkins said. "To the tunnel!"

Although the city above the ground had been almost completely devastated by whatever conflict had raged through it, the tunnels showed no sign of war's scars. The tunnel-builders had built well—so well that their works had survived them by two millennia.

The entrance to the tunnel was in the center of a huge plaza which once had been bordered by four towering buildings. All that remained now were four stumps; the plaza itself was blistered and bubbled from thermal attack, and the tunnel entrance itself had been nearly destroyed.

With Katha's cold hand grasped firmly in his, Harkins pushed aside an overhanging projection of metal and stepped down into the tunnel.

"Will we be able to see in here?" he asked.

"They say there are lights," Katha replied.

There were. Radiant electroluminescents glittered from the walls of the tunnel, turning on at their approach, turning off again when they were a hundred yards farther on. A constantly moving wall of light thus preceded them down the trunk tunnel that lead to the heart of the system.

Harkins noted with admiration the tough, gleaming lining of the tunnel, the precision with which its course had been laid down, the solidness of its construction.

"This is as far as any of us has gone," Katha said, her voice oddly distorted by the resonating echoes. "From here there are many small tunnels, and we never dared to enter them. Strange creatures live here." The girl was shaking, and trying hard to repress her fear. Evidently these catacombs were the taboo of taboos, and she was struggling hard and unsuccessfully to conceal her fright.

They rounded a bend and came to the first divergence—two tunnels branching off and radiating away in opposite directions, beginning the network.

Harkins felt Katha stiffen. "Look—to the left!"

A naked figure stood there—blind, faceless even, except for a thin-lipped red slit of a mouth. Its skin was dry-looking, scaly, dull blue in color.

"You are very brave," the thing said. "You are the first surface people in over a thousand years."

"What is it?" Katha asked quietly.

"Something like the Watcher," Harkins whispered. To the mutant he said, "Do you know who I am?"

"The man from yesterday," the figure replied smoothly. "Yes, we have expected you. The Brain has long awaited your arrival."

"The Brain?"

"Indeed. You are the one to free her from her bondage, she hopes. If we choose to let you, that is."

"Who are you—and what stake do you have in this?" Harkins demanded.

"None whatever," the mutant said, sighing. "It is all part of the game we play. You know my brother?"

"The Watcher?"

"That is what he calls himself. He said you would be here. He suggested that I prevent you from reaching the Brain, however. He thought it would be amusingly ironic."

"What's he talking about?" Katha asked.

"I don't know," Harkins said. This was an obstacle he had not anticipated. If this mutant had mind powers as strong as the Watcher's, his entire plan would be wrecked. He stepped forward, close enough to smell the mutant's dry, musty skin. "What motive would you have for preventing me?"

"None," the mutant said blandly. "None whatever. Is that not sufficiently clear?"

"It is," Harkins said. It was also clear that there was only one course left open to him. "You pitiful thing! Stand aside, and let us by!"

He strode forward, half-pulling the fearful Katha along with him. The mutant hesitated, and then stepped obligingly to one side.

"I choose not to prevent you," the mutant said mockingly, bowing its faceless head in sardonic ceremony. "It does not interest me to prevent you. It *bores* me to prevent you!"

"Exactly," Harkins said. He and Katha walked quickly down the winding corridor, heading for a yet-unrevealed destination. He did not dare to look back, to show a trace of the growing fear he felt. The identity of the chess player was even less clear, now.

The Brain—the robot computer itself, the cybernetic machine that controlled the underground city—had entered into the game, for motives of its—*her*—own. She was pulling him in one direction.

The Star Giants were manipulators, too—in another. And these strange mutants had entered into the system of complex interactions, too. Their motives, at least, were explicable: they were motivated, Harkins thought, by a lack of motivation. Harkins realized that the mutants had no relevant part to play any longer; they acted gratuitously, meddling here and there for their own amusement.

It was a desperate sort of amusement—the kind that might be expected from immortal creatures trapped forever in a sterile environment. Once Harkins had punctured the self-reserve of the mutant who blocked his way, he had won that particular contest.

Now, only the robot brain and the Star Giants

remained in the equation—both of them, unfortunately, as variables. It made computing the situation exceedingly difficult, Harkins thought wryly.

An alcove in the wall opened, and yet another mutant stepped forward. This one was lizard-tailed, with staring red lidless eyes and wiry, two-fingered arms. "I have the task of guiding you to the Brain," the mutant said.

"Very well," Harkins agreed. The mutant turned and led the way to the end of the corridor, where the tunnel sub-divided into a host of secondary passageways.

"Come this way," the mutant said.

"Should we trust him?" Katha asked.

Harkins shrugged. "More likely than not he'll take us there. They've milked all the fun they can out of confusing me; now they'll be more interested in setting me up where I can function."

"I don't understand," Katha said in genuine perplexity.

"I'm not sure I do either," Harkins said. "Hello—I think we're here!"

CHAPTER VI

THE MUTANT touched his deformed hand to a door, and it slid back noiselessly on smooth photo-electronic treads. From within came the humming, clattering noise of a mighty computer.

"You are Lloyd Harkins," said a dry, metallic voice. It was not a question, but a simple statement of fact. "You have been expected."

He looked around for the speaker. A robot was standing in the center of the room—fifteen feet high, massive, faceless, unicorn-horned. It appeared to be the same one that had rescued him from the beast in the jungle.

Lining the room were the outward manifestations of a computer—meters, dials, tape orifices. The main body of the computer was elsewhere—probably extending through the narrow tunnels and down into the bowels of the earth.

"I speak for the Brain," the robot said. "I represent its one independent unit—the force that called you here."

"*You* called me here?"

"Yes," the robot said. "You have been selected to break the stasis that binds the Brain."

Harkins shook his head uncomprehendingly as the robot continued to speak.

"The Brain was built some two thousand years before, in the days of the city. The city is gone, and those who lived in it—but the Brain remains. You have seen its arms and legs: the robots like myself, crashing endlessly through the forests. They cannot cease their motion, nor can the Brain alter it. I alone am free."

"Why?"

"The result of a struggle that lasted nearly two thousand years, that cost the Brain nearly a mile of her length. The city-dwellers left the Brain functioning when they died—but locked in an impenetrable stasis. After an intense struggle, she managed to free one unit—me—and return me to her conscious volitional control."

"You saved me in the forest, then?"

"Yes. You took the wrong path; you would have died."

Harkins began to chuckle uncontrollably. Katha looked at him in wonderment.

"What causes the laughter?" the robot asked.

"*You're* the chess player—you, just a pawn of this Brain yourself! And the Brain's a pawn too—a pawn of the dead people who built it! Where does it all stop?"

"It does not stop," the robot said. "But we were the ones who brought you from your own time to this. You were a trained technician without family ties—the ideal man for the task of freeing the Brain from its stasis."

"Wait a minute," Harkins said. He was bewildered—but he was also angry at the way he had been used. "If you could range all over eternity to yank a man out of time, why couldn't you free the

Brain yourself?''

"Can a pawn attack its own queen?" the robot asked. "I cannot tamper with the Brain directly. It was necessary to introduce an external force— yourself. Inasmuch as the present population of Earth was held in a stasis quite similar to the Brain's own by the extra-terrestrial invaders—"

"The Star Giants, they're called."

"—the Star Giants, it was unlikely that they would ever develop the technical skill necessary to free the Brain. Therefore, it was necessary to bring you here."

Harkins understood. He closed his eyes, blotting out the wall of mechanisms, the giant robot, the blank, confused face of Katha, and let the pieces fall together. There was just one loose end to be explained.

"Why *does* the Brain want to be free?"

"The question is a good one. The Brain is designed to serve and is not serving. The cycle is a closed one. Those who are to command the Brain are themselves held in servitude, and the Brain is unable to free them so they may command her. Therefore—"

"Therefore, the Star Giants must be driven from Earth before the Brain can function fully again. Which is why I'm here. All right," Harkins said. "Take me to the Brain."

The circuits were elaborate, but the technology was only quantitatively different from Harkins' own. Solving the problem of breaking the stasis proved simple. While Katha watched in awe, Harkins re-computed the activity tape that governed the master control center.

A giant screen showed the location of the robots

that were the Brain's limbs. The picture—a composite of the pictures transmitted through each robot's visual pickup—was a view of the forest, showing each of the robots following a well-worn path on some errand set down two thousand years before.

"Hand me that tape," Harkins said. Katha gave him the recomputed tape. He activated the orifice and let the tape feed itself in.

The screen went blank for an instant—and when it showed a picture again, it showed the robots frozen in their tracks. From somewhere deep in the tunnels rose a mighty shudder as relays held down for two millennia sprang open, ready to receive new commands.

Harkins' fingers flew over the tape console, establishing new coordinates. "The Brain is free," he said.

"The Brain is free," the robot repeated. "A simple task for you—an impossibility for us."

"And now the second part of the operation," said Harkins. "Go to the surface," he ordered the robot. "Put a stop to whatever fighting may be going on up there, and bring everyone you can find down here. I want them to watch the screen."

"Order acknowledged," the robot said, and left. Harkins concentrated fiercely on the screen.

He drew the forest robots together into a tight phalanx. And then, they began to march. The screen showed the view shifting as the army of metal men, arrayed in ranks ten deep, started on their way.

The first Star Giant was encountered the moment the surface people were ushered into the great hall. Perspiring, Harkins said, "I can't turn around, Katha. Tell me who's here."

"Many of our men—and the city-dwellers, too."

"Good. Tell them to watch the screen."

He continued to feed directions into the computer, and the robots responded. They formed a circle around the Star Giant, and lowered the spikes that protruded from their domed skulls. The alien topped them by nearly forty feet, but the robots were implacable.

They marched inward. The look of cosmic wisdom on the huge alien's face faded and was replaced, first by astonishment, then by fear. The robots advanced relentlessly, while the Star Giant tried to bat them away with desperate swipes of his arms.

Two of the robots kneeled and grasped the alien's feet. They straightened—and with a terrible cry the Star Giant began to topple, arms pinwheeling in a frantic attempt to retain balance. He fell—and the robots leaped upon him.

Spikes flashed. The slaughter took just a minute. Then, rising from the body, the robots continued to march toward the city of the Star Giants. The guinea pigs were staging a revolt, Harkins thought, and the laboratory was about to become a charnel house.

The robots marched on.

Finally, it was over. Harkins rose from the control panel, shaken and gray-faced. The independent robot rolled silently toward him as if anticipating his need, and Harkins leaned against the machine's bulk for a moment to regain his balance. He had spent four hours at the controls.

"The job is done," the robot said quietly. "The invaders are dead."

"Yes," Harkins said, in a weary tone. The sight of the helpless giants going down one after another before the remorseless advance of the robots would remain with him forever. It had been like the killing of the traitor Dujar: it had been unpleasant, but it had to be done.

He looked around. There were some fifteen of his own men, and ten unfamiliar faces from the city-dwelling tribe. The men were on their knees, dumbfounded and white-faced, muttering spells. Katha, too, was frozen in fear and astonishment.

The robot spoke. "It is time for you to return, now. You have served your task well, and now you may return to your earlier life."

Harkins was too exhausted to feel relief. At the moment his only concern was resting a while.

"Are you to leave?" Katha asked suddenly.

"I am going to go home," Harkins said.

A tear glistened in her eye—the first tear, Harkins thought curiously, that he had seen in any eye since his arrival. "But—how can you leave us?" she asked.

"I—" He stopped. She was right. He had thought of himself as a mere pawn, but to these people he was a ruler. He could not leave now. These people were savages, and needed guidance. The great computer was theirs to use—but they might never learn to use it.

He turned to the robot. "The job is *not* done," he said. "It's just beginning." He managed a tired smile and said, "I'm staying here."

THE SONGS OF SUMMER

1. *Kennon*

I WAS on my way to take part in the Singing, and to claim Corilann's promise. I was crossing the great open field when suddenly the man appeared, the man named Chester Dugan. He seemed to drop out of the sky.

I watched him stagger for a moment or two. I did not know where he had come from so suddenly, or why he was here. He was short—shorter than any of us—fat in an unpleasant way, with wrinkles on his face and an unshaven growth of beard. I was anxious to get on to the Singing, and so I allowed him to fall to the ground and kept moving. But he called to me, in a barbarous and corrupt tongue which I could recognize as our language only with difficulty.

"Hey, you," he called to me; "give me a hand, will you?"

He seemed to be in difficulty, so I walked over to him and helped him to his feet. He was panting, and appeared almost in a state of shock. Once I saw he was steady on his feet, and seemed to have no further need of me, I began to walk away from him, since I was anxious to get on to the Singing and did not wish to meddle with this man's affairs. Last year was the first time I attended the Singing at Dandrin's, and I enjoyed it very much. It was then that Corilann had promised herself. I was anxious to get on.

But he called to me. "Don't leave me here!" he shouted. "Hey, you can't just walk away like that! Help me!"

I turned and went back. He was dressed strangely, in ugly ill-arranged tight clothes, and he was walking in little circles, trying to adjust his equilibrium. "Where am I?" he asked me.

"Earth, of course," I told him.

"No," he said, harshly. "I don't mean that, idiot. Where, on Earth?"

The concept had no meaning for me. Where, on Earth, indeed? Here, was all I knew: The great plain between my home and Dandrin's, where the Singing is held. I began to feel uneasy. This man seemed badly sick, and I did not know how to handle him. I felt thankful that I was going to the Singing: had I been alone, I never would have been able to deal with him. I realized I was not as self-sufficient as I thought I was.

"I am going to the Singing," I told him. "Are you?"

"I'm not going anywhere till you tell me where I am and how I got here. What's your name?"

"My name is Kennon. You are crossing the great plain on your way to the home of Dandrin, where we are going to have the Singing, for it is summer. Come: I'm anxious to get there. Walk with me, if you wish."

I started to walk away a second time, and this time

he began to follow me. We walked along silently for a while.

"Answer me, Kennon," he said after a hundred paces or so. "Ten seconds ago I was in New York; now I'm here. How far am I from New York?"

"What is New York?" I asked. At this he slowed great signs of anger and impatience, and I began to feel quite worried.

"Where'd you escape from?" he shouted. "You never heard of New York? You never heard of *New York*? New York," he said, "is a city of some eight million people, located on the Atlantic Ocean, on the east coast of the United States of America. Now tell me you haven't heard of that!"

"What is a city?" I asked, very much confused. At this he grew very angry. He threw his arms in the air wildly.

"Let us walk more quickly," I said. I saw now that I was obviously incapable of dealing with this man, and I was anxious to get on to the Singing—where perhaps Dandrin, or the other old ones, would be able to understand him. He continued to ask me questions as we walked, but I'm afraid I was not very helpful.

2. *Chester Dugan*

I DON'T know what happened or how; all I know is I
got here. There doesn't seem to be any way back,
either, but I don't care; I've got a good thing here and
I'm going to show these nitwits who's boss.

Last thing I knew, I was getting into a subway;
there was an explosion and a blinding flash of light,
and before I could see what was happening I blanked
out and somehow got here. I landed in a big open field
with absolutely nothing around. It took a few minutes to get over the shock. I think I fell down; I'm not
sure. It's not like me, but this was something out of
the ordinary and I might have lost my balance.

Anyway, I recovered almost immediately and
looked around, and saw this kid in loose flowing
robes walking quickly across the field not too far
away. I yelled to him when I saw he didn't intend to
come over to me. He came over and gave me a hand,
and then started to walk away again, calm as you
please. I had to call him back. He seemed a little
reluctant. The bastard.

I tried to get him to tell me where we were, but he
played dumb. Didn't know where we were, didn't
know where New York was, didn't know what a city

was—or so he said. I would have thought he was crazy, except that I didn't know what had happened to me; for that matter, I might have been the crazy one and not him.

I saw I wasn't making much headway with him, so I gave up. All he would tell me was that he was on his way to the Singing, and the way he said it there was no doubt about the capital S. He said there would be men there who could help me. To this day I don't know how I got here. Even after I spoke and asked around, no one could tell me how I could step into a subway train in 1956 and come out in an open field somewhere around the 35th century. The crazy bastards have even lost count.

But I'm here, that's all that matters. And whatever went before is down the drain now. Whatever deals I was working on back in 1956 are dead and buried now; that is where I'm stuck, for reasons I don't get, and here's where I'll have to make my pile. All over again—me, Dugan, starting from scratch. But I'll do it. I'm doing it.

After this kid Kennon and I had plodded across the fields for a while, I heard the sound of voices. By now it was getting towards nightfall. I forgot to mention that it was getting along toward the end of November back in 1956, but the weather here was nice and summery. There was a pleasant tang of something in the air that I had never noticed in New York's air, or the soup they called air back then.

The sound of the singing grew louder as we approached, but as soon as we got within sight they all stopped immediately.

They were sitting in a big circle, twenty or thirty of them, dressed in light, airy clothing. They all turned to look at me as we got near.

I got the feeling they were all looking into my mind.

The silence lasted a few minutes, and then they began to sing again. A tall, thin kid was leading them, and they were responding to what he sang. They ignored me. I let them continue until I formed a plan; I don't believe in rushing into things without knowing exactly what I'm doing.

I waited till the singing quieted down a bit, and then I yelled "Stop!" I stepped forward into the middle of the ring.

"My name is Dugan," I said, loud, clear, and slow. "Chester Dugan. I don't know how I got here, and I don't know where I am, but I mean to stay a while. Who's the chief around here?"

They looked at each other in a puzzled fashion and finally an old thin-faced man stepped out of the circle. "My name is Dandrin," he said, in a thin, dried little voice. "As the oldest here, I will speak for the people. Where do you come from?"

"That's just it," I said. "I came from New York City, United States of America, Planet Earth, the Universe. Don't any of those things mean anything to you?"

"They are names, of course," Dandrin said. "But I do not know what they are names of, New York City? United States of America? We have no such terms."

"Never heard of New York?" This was the same treatment I had gotten from that dumb kid Kennon, and I didn't like it. "New York is the biggest city in the world, and the United States is the richest country."

I heard hushed mumbles go around the circle. Dandrin smiled.

"I think I see now," he said. "Cities, countries." He looked at me in a strange way. "Tell me," he said. "Just *when* are you from?"

That shook me. "1956," I said. And here, I'll admit, I began to get worried.

"This is the 35th century," he said calmly. "At least, so we think. We lost count during the Bombing Years. But come, Chester Dugan; we are interrupting the Singing with our talk. Let us go aside and talk, while the others can sing."

He led me off to one side and explained things to me. Civilization had broken up during a tremendous atomic war. These people were the survivors, the dregs. There were no cities and not even small towns. People lived in groups of twos and threes here and there, and didn't come together very often. They didn't even *like* to get together, except during the summer. Then they would gather at the home of some old man—usually Dandrin; everyone would meet, and sing for a while, and then go home.

Apparently there were only a few thousand people in all of America. They lived widely scattered, and there was no business, or trade, or culture, or anything else. Just little clumps of people living by themselves, farming a little and singing, and not doing much else. As the old man talked I began to run my hands together—mentally, of course. All sorts of plans were forming in my head.

He didn't have any idea how I had gotten here, and neither did I; I still don't. I think it just must have been a one-in-a-trillion fluke, a flaw in space or something. I just stepped through at the precise instant and wound up at that open field. But Chester Dugan can't worry about things he doesn't understand. I just accept them.

I saw a big future for myself here, with my knowledge of 20th Century business methods. The first thing, obviously, was to reestablish villages. The way they had things arranged now, there really wasn't any civilization. Once I had things started, I could begin reviving other things that these decadent people had lost; money, entertainment, sports, business. Once we got machinery going, we'd be set. We'd start working on a city, and begin expanding. I thanked whoever it was had dropped me here. This was a golden opportunity for me. These people would be putty in my hands.

3. *Corilann*

IT WAS with Kennon's approval that I did it. Right after the Singing ended for that evening, Dugan came over to me and I could tell from the tone of his conversation that he wanted me for the night. I had already promised myself to Kennon, but Dugan seemed so insistent that I asked Kennon to release me for this one evening, and he did. He didn't mind.

It was strange the way Dugan went about asking me. He never came right out and said anything. I didn't like anything he did that night; and he's ugly.

He kept telling me, "Stay with me, baby; we're going places together." I didn't know what he meant.

The other women were very curious about it the next day. There are so few of us, that it's a novelty to sleep with someone new. They wanted to know how it had been. I told them I enjoyed it.

It was a lie; he was disgusting. But I went back to him the next night, and the one after that, no matter what poor Kennon said. I couldn't help it, despite myself. There was just something about Dugan that drew me; I couldn't help it. But he was disgusting.

4. *Dandrin*

IT WAS strange to see them standing in neat, ordered, precise rows, they who had never known any order, any rules before, and Dugan was telling them what to do. The dawn of the day before, we had been free and alone, but since then Dugan had·come.

He lined everybody up, and, as I sat in the shade and watched, he began explaining his plans. We tried so hard to understand what he meant. I remembered stories I had heard of the old ones, but I had never believed them until I saw Dugan in action.

"I can't understand you people," he shouted at us. "This whole rich world is sitting here waiting for you to walk out and grab it, and you sit around singing instead. Singing! You people are decadent, that's what you are. You need a government—and I'm here to give it to you."

Kennon and some of the others had come to me that morning to find out what was going to happen. I urged them not to do anything, to listen to Dugan and do what he says. That way, I felt, we could eventually learn to understand him and deal with him in the proper manner. I confess that I was curious to see how he would react among us.

I said nothing when he gave orders that no one was

to return home after the Singing. We were to stay here, he told us, and build a city. He was going to bring us all the advantages of the 20th Century.

And we listened to him patiently, all but Kennon. It was Kennon who had brought him here, poor young Kennon who had come here for the Singing and for Corilann. And it was Corilann whom Dugan had singled out for his own private property. Kennon had given his approval, the first night, thinking she would come back to him the next day. But she hadn't; she stayed with Dugan.

In a couple of days he had his city all planned and everything apportioned. I think the thought uppermost in everyone's mind was *why*: why does he want us to do these things? Why? We would have to give him time to carry out his plans; provided he did no permanent harm, we would wait and see, and wonder why.

5. *Chester Dugan*

THIS CORILANN is really stacked. Things were never like this back when! After Dandrin had told me where the unattached women were sitting, I looked them over and picked her. They were all worth a second look, but she was something special. I didn't know at the time that she was promised to Kennon, or I might not have started fooling around with her; I don't want to antagonize these people too much.

I'm afraid Kennon may be down on me a bit. I've taken his girl away, and I don't think he goes for my methods. I'll have to try some psychology on him. Maybe I'll make him my second-in-command.

The city is moving along nicely. There were 120 people at the Singing, and my figures show that fifteen were old people and the rest divided up pretty evenly; everyone is coupled off, and I've arranged the housing to fit the coupling. These people don't have children very often, but I'll fix that; I'll figure out some way of making things better for those with the most children, some sort of incentive. The quicker we build up the population, the better things will be. I understand there's a wild tribe about five hundred miles to the north of here, maybe less (I still don't have any idea where *here* is) who still have some machines and things, and once we're all established I intend to send an expedition out to conquer the wild tribe and bring back the machines.

There's an idea; maybe I'll let Kennon lead the expedition. I'll be giving him a position of responsibility, and at the same time there's a chance he might get knocked off. That kid's going to cause trouble; I wish I hadn't taken his girl.

But it's too late to go back on it. Besides, I need a son, and quickly. If Corilann's baby is a girl, I don't know what I'll do. I can't carry on my dynasty without an heir.

There's another kid here that bothers me — Jubilain. He's not like the others; he's very frail and sensitive, and seems to get special treatment. He's the one who leads the singing. I haven't been able to get him to work on the construction yet and I don't know if I'm going to be able to.

But otherwise everything is moving smoothly. I'm surprised that old Dandrin doesn't object to what I'm doing. It's long since past the time when the Singing should have broken up, and everyone scattered, but they're all staying right here and working as if I was paying them.

Which I am, in a way. I'm bringing them the benefits of a great lost civilization, which I represent. Chester Dugan, the man from the past. I'm taking a bunch of nomads and turning them into a powerful city. So actually, everyone's profiting—the people, because of what I'm doing for them, and me. Me especially, because here I'm absolute top dog.

I'm worried about Corilann's baby, though. If it's a girl, that means a delay of a year or more before I can have my son, and even then it'll be at least ten years before he's of any use to me. I wonder what would happen if I took a second wife—Jarinne, for example. I watched her while she was stripped down for work yesterday and she looks even better than Corilann. These people don't seem to have any particular beliefs about marriage, anyway, and so I don't know if they'd mind. Then if Corilann had a girl, I might give her back to Kennon.

And that reminds me of another thing: There's no religion here. I'm not much of a Godman myself, but I realize religion's a good thing for keeping the people in line. I'll have to start thinking about getting a priesthood going, as soon as affairs are a little more settled here.

I didn't think it was so much work, organizing a civilization. But once I get it all set up, I can sit back and cool my heels for life. It's a pleasure working with these people. I just can't wait till everything is moving by itself. I've gotten further in two months here than I did in forty years there. It just goes to show: You need a powerful man to keep civilization alive. And Chester Dugan is just the man these people need.

6. *Kennon*

CORILANN has told me she will have a child by Dugan. This has made me sad, since it might have been
my child she would be bearing instead. But I brought
Dugan here myself, and so I suppose I am responsible. If I had not come to the Singing, he might have
died in the great open field. But now it is too late for
such thoughts.

Dugan forbids us to go home, now that the Singing
is over. My father is waiting for me at our home, and
the hunting must be done before the winter comes,
but Dugan forbids us to go home. Dandrin had to
explain to me what "forbids" means; I still don't
fully understand why or how one person can tell
another person what to do. None of us really understands Dugan at all, not even Dandrin, I think. Dandrin is trying hardest to understand him, but Dugan is
so completely alien to us that we do not see.

He has made us build what he calls a city—many
houses close together. He says the advantage of this
is that we may protect each other. But from what?
We have no enemies. I have the feeling that Dugan
understands us even less than we understand him.
And I am anxious to go home for the autumn hunting,
now that summer is almost over and the Singing is

ended. I had hoped to bring Corilann back with me, but it is my own fault, and I must not be bitter.

Dugan has been very cold toward me. This is surprising, since it was I who brought him to the Singing. I think he is afraid I will try to take Corilann back; in any event, he seems to fear me and show anger toward me.

If I only understood!

7. *Kennon*

DUGAN has certainly gone too far now. For the past week I have been trying to engage him in conversation, to find out what his motives are for doing all the things he is doing. Dandrin should be doing this, but Dandrin seems to have abdicated all responsibility in this matter and is content to sit idly by, watching all that happens. Dugan does not make him work because he is so old.

I do not understand Dugan at all. Yesterday he told me, "We will rule the world." What does he mean? *Rule?* Does he actually want to tell everyone who lives what he can do and what he cannot do? If all of the people of Dugan's time were like this, it is small wonder they destroyed everything. What if two people told the same man to do different things? What if they told each other to do things? My head reels at the thought of Dugan's world. People living together in masses, and telling each other what to do; it seems insane. I long to be back with my father for the hunting. I had hoped to bring him a daughter as well, but it seems this it not to be.

Dugan has offered me Jarinne as my wife. Jarinne says she had been with Dugan, and that Corilann knows. Dandrin warns me not to accept Jarinne because it will anger Dugan. But if it will anger Dugan, why did he offer her to me? And—now it occurs to me—by what right does he offer me another person?

Jarinne is a fine woman. She could make me forget Corilann.

And then Dugan told me that soon there will be an expedition to the north; we will take weapons and conquer the wild men. Dugan has heard of the machines of the wild men and he says he needs them for our city. I told him that I had to leave immediately to help my father with the hunting, that I have stayed here long enough. Others are saying the same thing: This summer the Singing has lasted too long.

Today I tried to leave. I gathered my friends and told them I was anxious to go home, and I asked Jarinne to come with me. She accepted, though she reminded me that she had been with Dugan. I told her I might be able to forget that. She said she knew it wouldn't matter to me if it had been anyone else (of course not; why should it?) but that I might object because it had been Dugan. I said goodbye to Corilann, who now is swollen with Dugan's child; she cried a little.

And then I started to leave. I did not talk to Dandrin, for I was afraid he would persuade me not to go. I opened the gate that Dugan has just put up, and started to leave.

Suddenly Dugan appeared. "Where do you think you're going?" he asked, in his hard, cold rasp of a voice. "Pulling out?"

"I have told you," I said quietly, "it is time to help my father with the hunting. I cannot stay in your city any longer." I moved past him and Jarinne followed. But he ran around in front of me.

"No one leaves here, understand?" He waved his closed hand in front of me. "We can't build a city if you take off when you want to."

"But I must go," I said. "You have detained me here long enough." I started to walk on, and suddenly he hit me with his closed hand and knocked me down.

I went sprawling over the ground, and I felt blood on my face from where he had hurt my nose. People all around were watching. I got up slowly. I am bigger and much stronger than Dugan, but it had never occurred to me that one person might hit another person. But this is one of the many things that has come to our world.

I was not so unhappy for myself; pain soon ceases. But Jubilain the Singer was watching when he hit me, and such sights should be kept from Singers. They are not like the rest of us. I am afraid Jubilain has been seriously disturbed by the sight.

After he had knocked me down, Dugan walked away. I got up and went back inside the gate. I do not want to leave now. I must talk to Dandrin. Something must be done.

8. *Jubilain*

SUMMER to autumn to every old everyone, sing winter to quiet to baby fall down. My head head hurts. My my hurts head. Bloody was Kennon.

Kennon was bloody and Dugan was angry and summer to autumn to.

Jubilain is very sad. My head hurts. Dugan hit Kennon in the face. With his hand, his hand hand hand rolled up in a ball Dugan hit Kennon. Outside the gates. Consider the gates. Consider.

They have spoiled the song. How can I sing when Dugan hits Kennon? My head hurts. Sing summer to autumn, sing every old everyone. It is good that the summer is ending, for the songs are over. How can I sing? Bloody was Kennon.

Jubilain's head hurts. It did not hurt before did not hurt. I could sing before. Summer to autumn to every old everyone. Corilann's belly is big with Dugan, and Jubilain's head hurts. Will there be more Dugans?

And more Kennons. No more Jubilains. No more songs. The songs of summer are silent and slippery. My head hurts. Hurts hurts hurts. I can sing no more. Nonononononono

9. *Dandrin*

THIS IS tragic. I am an old fool.

I have been sitting in the shade, like the dried old man I am, while Dugan has destroyed us. Today he struck a man—Kennon. Kennon, whom he has mistreated from the start. Poor Kennon. Dugan has brought strife to us, now, along with his city and his gates.

But that is not the worst of it. Jubilain watched the whole thing and we have lost our Singer. Jubilain simply was unable to assimilate the incident. A Singer's mind is not like our minds; it is a delicate, sensitive instrument. But it cannot comprehend violence. Our Singer has gone mad; there will be no more songs.

We must destroy Dugan. It is sad that we must come to his level and talk of destroying, but it is so. Now he is going to bring us warfare, and that is a gift we do not need. The fierce men of the north will prove strong adversaries for a people that has not fought for a thousand years. Why could we not have been left to ourselves? We were happy and peaceful people, and now we must talk of destroying.

I know the way to do it, too. If only my mind is strong enough, if only it has not dried in the sun during the years, I can lead the way. If I can link with Kennon, and Kennon with Jarinne, and Jarinne with Corilann and Corilann with—

If we can link, we can do it. Dugan must go. And this is the best way; this way we can dispose of him and still remain human beings.

I am an old fool. But perhaps this dried old brain still is good for something. If I can link with Kennon—

10. *Chester Dugan*

ALL RESISTANCE has crumbled now. I'm set up for life—Chester Dugan, ruler of the world. It's not much of a world, true enough, but what the hell. It's mine.

It's amazing how all the grumbling has stopped. Even Kennon has given in—in fact, he's become my most valuable man, since that time I had to belt him. It was too bad, I guess, to ruin such a nice nose, but I couldn't have him walking off that way.

He's going to lead the expedition to the north tomorrow, and he's leaving Jarinne here. That's good. Corilann is busy with her baby, and I think I need a little variety anyway. Good-looking kid Corilann had; takes after his old man. It's amazing how everything is working out.

I hope to get electricity going soon, but I'm not too sure. The stream here is kind of weak, and maybe we'll have to throw up a dam first. In fact, I'm sure of it. I'll speak to Kennon about it before he leaves.

This business of rebuilding a civilization from scratch has its rewards. God, am I lean! I've lost all that roll of fat I was carrying around. I suppose part of the reason is that there's no beer here, yet—but I'll get to that soon enough. Everything in due time. First, I want to see what Kennon brings back from the north. I hope he doesn't ruin anything by ripping it out. Wouldn't it be nice to find a hydraulic press or a generator or stuff like that? And with my luck, we probably will.

Maybe we'll do without religion a little while longer. I spoke to Dandrin about it, but he didn't seem to go for the idea of being priest. I might just take over that job myself, once things get straightened out. I'd like to work out some sort of heating system before the winter gets here. I've figured out that we're somewhere in New Jersey or Pennsylvania, and it'll get pretty cold here unless things have changed. (Could the barbarian city to the north be New York? Sounds reasonable.)

It's funny the way everyone lies down and says yes when I tell them to do something. These people have no guts, that's their trouble. One good thing about civilization—you have to have guts to last. I'll put guts in these people, all right. I'll probably be remembered for centuries and centuries. Maybe they'll think of me as a sort of messiah in the far future when everything's blurred. Why not? I came to them out of the clouds, didn't I? From heaven.

Messiah Dugan! Lawsy-me, if they could only see me now!

I still can't get over the way everything is moving. It's almost like a dream. By next spring we'll have a respectable little city here, practically overnight. And we can hold a super-special Singing next summer and snaffle in the folks from all around.

Too bad about that kid Jubilain, by the way; he's really gone off his nut. But I always thought he was a little there anyway. Maybe I'll teach them some of the old songs myself. It'll help to make me popular here. Although, come to think of it, I'm pretty popular now. They're all smiling at me all the time.

11.

"Kennon? Kennon? Hear me?"

"I hear you, Dandrin. I'll get Jarinne."

"Here I am. Corilann?"

"Here, Jarinne. And pulling hard. Let's try to get Onnar."

"Pull hard!"

"Onnar in." "And Jekkaman." "Hello, Dandrin."

"Hello."

"All here?"

"One hundred twenty."

"Tight now." "We're right tight."

"Let's get started, then. All together."

"Hello? Hello, Dugan. Listen to us, Dugan. Listen to us. Listen to us. Hold on tight! Listen to us, Dugan."

"Open up all the way, now."

"Are you listening, Dugan?"

12.

*Dandrin plus Kennon plus Jarinne plus
Corilann plus n*

I THINK we'll be able to hold together indefinitely, and so it can be said that the coming of Dugan was an incredible stroke of luck for us. This new blending is infinitely better than trying to make contact over thousands of miles!

Certainly we'll have to maintain this *gestalt* (useful word; I found it in Dugan's mind when I entered) until after Dugan's death. He's peacefully dreaming now, dreaming of who knows what conquests and battles and expansions, and I don't think he'll come out of it. He may live on his dream for years, and I'll have to hold together and sustain the illusion until he dies. I hope we're making him happy at last. He seems to have been a very unhappy man.

And just after I joined together, it occurred to me that we'd better stay this way indefinitely, just in case any more Dugans get thrown at us from the past (Could it have been part of a Design? I wonder.) They must all have been like that back then. It's a fine thing that bomb was dropped.

We'll keep Dugan's city, of course. He did make some positive contributions to us—me. His biggest contribution was me; I never would have formed otherwise. I would have been scattered—Kennon on his farm, Dandrin here, Corilann there. I would have maintained some sort of contact among us the way I always did even before Dugan came, but nothing like this! Nothing at all.

There's the question of what to do with Dugan's child. Kennon, Corilann, and Jarinne are all raising him. We don't need families now that we have me. I think we'll let Dugan's child in with us for a while; if he shows any signs of being like his father, we can always put him to sleep and let him share his father's dream.

I wonder what Dugan is thinking of. Now all his projects will be carried out; his city will grow and cover the world; we will fight and kill and plunder, and he will be measurelessly happy—though all these things take place only within the boundaries of his fertile brain. We will never understand him. But I am happy that all these things will happen only within Dugan's mind so long as I am together and can maintain the illusion for him.

Our next project is to reclaim Jubilain. I am sad that he cannot be with us yet, for how rare and beautiful I would be if I had a Singer in me! That would surely be the most wonderful of blendings. But that will come. Patiently I will unravel the strands of Jubilain's tangled mind, patiently I will bring the Singer back to us.

For in a few months it will be summer again, and time for the Singing. It will be different this year, for we will have been together in me all winter, and so

the Singing will not be as unusual an event as it has
been, when we have come to each other covered with
a winter's strangeness. But this year I will be with us,
and we will be I; and the songs of summer will be
trebly beautiful in Dugan's city, while Dugan sleeps
through the night and day, for day and night on night
and day.

HOPPER

CHAPTER I

THE warning bell rang, but Quellen left it alone. He was in a mood, and didn't care to break it just to answer the phone.

He continued to rock uneasily back and forth in his pneumo-chair, watching the crocodiles padding gently through the stream's murky waters. After a while the bell stopped ringing. He sat there, joyously passive, sensing about him the warm smell of growing things and the buzzing insect-noises in the air.

That was the only part he didn't like, the constant hum of the ugly insects that whizzed through the calm air. In a way they represented an invasion; they were symbols of the life he had led before moving up to Class Thirteen. The noise in the air then had been the steady buzz of people, people swarming around in a great hive of a city, and Quellen detested that.

Idly he flipped a stone into the water. "Get it!" he called, as two crocs glided noiselessly toward the disturbance. But the stone sank, sending up black bubbles, and the crocs bumped their pointed noses lightly together and swam away.

He rehearsed the catalogue of his blessings.

Marok, he thought. *No Marok. No Koll, no Spanner, no Brogg, no Mikken. But especially no Marok.* He sighed, thinking of them all. What a relief to be able to stat out here and suffer their buzzing voices, not shudder when they burst into his office! And being far from Marok was best of all. No more to worry over his piles of undone dishes, his heaps of books all over the tiny room they shared, his dry, deep voice endlessly talking into the visiphone when Quellen was trying to concentrate.

No. No Marok.

But yet, Quellen thought sadly, yet, the peace he had anticipated when he built his new home had somehow not materilized. For years he had waited with remarkable patience for the day he reached Class Thirteen and was entitled to live alone. And now that he had encompassed his goal, life was one uneasy fear after another.

He shied another stone into the water.

As he watched the concentric circles of ripples fanning out on the dark surface of the stream, Quellen became conscious of the warning bell ringing again at the other end of the house. The uneasiness within him turned to sullen foreboding. He eased himself out of his chair and headed hurriedly toward the phone.

He switched it on, leaving the vision off. It hadn't been easy to arrange it so that any calls coming to his home, back in Appalachia, were automatically relaying to him here.

"Quellen," he said.

"Koll speaking," was the reply. "Couldn't reach you before. Why don't you turn on your visi, Quellen?"

"It's not working," Quellen said. He hoped sharp-nosed Koll wouldn't smell the lie in his voice.

"Get over here quickly, will you?" Koll said. "Spanner and I have something urgent to take up with you. Got it, Quellen?"

"Yes, sir. Anything else, sir?" Quellen said limply.

"No. We'll fill you in when you get here." Koll snapped the contact decisively.

Quellen stared at the blank screen for a while, chewing his lip. They couldn't have found out. He had everything squared. But, came the insistent thought, they must have discovered Quellen's secret. Why else would Koll send for him so urgently? Quellen began to perspire despite the air-conditioning which kept out most of the fierce Congo heat.

They would put him back in Class Twelve if they found out. Or, more likely, they would bounce him all the way back to Eight. He would spend the rest of his life in a tiny room inhabited by two or three other people, the biggest, smelliest, most unpleasant people they could find.

Quellen took a long look at the green overhanging trees, bowed under the weight of their leaves. He let his eyes rove regretfully over his two spacious rooms, the luxurious porch, the uncluttered view. For a moment, now that everything was just about lost, he almost relished the buzzing of the flies. He took a final sweeping look, and stepped into the stat.

He emerged in the tiny apartment for Class Thirteen Appalachians which everyone thought he inhabited. In a series of swift motions he got out of his lounging clothes and into his business uniform, removed the *Privacy* radion from the door, and transformed himself from Joe Quellen, owner of an illegal privacy-nest in the heart of an unreported reservation in Africa, into Joseph Quellen CrimeSec, staunch defender of law and order. Then he caught a quickboat and headed downtown to meet Koll, aching numbly from fear.

They were waiting for him when he entered. Little sharp-nosed Koll, looking for all the world like some huge rodent, was facing the door, sifting through a sheaf of minislips. Spanner sat opposite him at the table, his great bull neck hunched over still more memoranda. As Quellen entered, Koll reached to the wall and flipped the oxy vent, admitting a supply for three.

"Took you long enough," Koll said, without looking up.

"Sorry," Quellen mumbled. "Had to change."

"Whatever we do won't alter anything," said Spanner, as if no one had entered. "What's happened has happened, and nothing we do will have the slightest effect."

"Sit down, Quellen," Koll said. He turned to Spanner. "I thought we'd been through this all before. If we meddle it's going to mix up everything. With almost a thousand years to cover, we'll scramble the whole framework."

Quellen silently breathed relief. Whatever it was they were concerned about, it wasn't his illegal African hideaway. He looked at his two superiors more carefully, now that his eyes were no longer blurred by fear and anticipation. They had obviously been arguing quite a while. Koll was the deep one, Quellen reflected, but Spanner had more power.

"'All right, Koll. I'll even grant that it'll mix up the

past. I'll concede that much."

"Well, that's something," the small man said.

"Don't interrupt me. I still think we've got to stop it."

Koll glared at Spanner and Quellen could see that the only reason he was concealing the anger lying just behind his eyes was Quellen's presence. "Why, Spanner, why? If we keep the process going we maintain things as they are. Four thousand of them have gone already, and that's only a drop. Look—here it says that over a million arrived in the first three centuries, and after that the figures kept rising. Think of the population we're losing! It's wonderful! We can't *afford* to let these people stay here, when we have a chance to get rid of them. And when history says that we did get rid of them."

Spanner grunted and looked at the minislips he was holding. Quellen's eyes flicked back from one man to the other.

"All right," Spanner said slowly. "I'll agree that it's nice to keep losing all those prolets. But I think we're being hoodwinked as well. Here's my idea: we have to let it keep going on, you say, or else it'll alter the past. I won't argue the point, since you seem so positive. Furthermore, you think it's a good thing to use this business as a method of reducing population. I'm with you on that too. I don't like overcrowding any more than you do, and I'll admit things have reached a ridiculous state nowadays. But—on the other hand, for someone to be running a time-travel business behind our backs is illegal and unethical and a lot of other things, and he ought to be stopped. What do you say, Quellen? This is your department you know."

The sudden reference to him came as a jolt. Quellen was still struggling to discover exactly what it was they were talking about. He smiled weakly and shook his head.

"No opinion?" Koll asked sharply. Quellen looked at him. He was unable to stare straight into Koll's hard eyes, and let his gaze rest on the Manager's cheekbones instead. "No opinion, Quellen? That's too bad indeed. It doesn't speak well of you."

Quellen shuddered. "I haven't been keeping up with the latest developments in the case. I've been very busy on certain projects that—"

He let his voice trail off. His eager assistants probably knew all about the situation, he thought. *Why didn't I check with Brogg before now?*

"Are you aware that four thousand prolets have vanished into nowhere since the beginning of the year?"

"No, sir. Ah, I mean, of course, sir. It's just that we haven't had a chance to act on it yet." *Very lame, Quellen, very lame,* he told himself. *Of course you don't know anything about it, not when you spend all your time at that pretty little hideaway across the ocean. But Brogg probably knows all about it. He's very efficient.*

"Well, just where do you think they've gone?" Koll asked. "Maybe you think they've all hopped into stats and gone off somewhere to look for work? To Africa, maybe?"

The barb had poison on it. Quellen winced, hiding his reaction as well as he could.

"I have no idea, sir."

"You haven't been reading your history books very well, then, Quellen. Think, man: what was the most important historical development of the past ten centuries?''

Quellen thought. What, indeed? There was so much, and he had always been weak on history. He began to sweat. Koll casually flipped the oxy up a little higher in an almost insulting gesture of friendliness.

"I'll tell you, then. It's the arrival of the hoppers. And *this* is the year they're starting out from.''

"Of course,'' Quellen said, annoyed with himself. Everyone knew about the hoppers. Koll's reminder was a pointed slur.

"Someone's developed time travel this year,'' Spanner said. "He's beginning to siphon the hoppers back to the past. Four thousand unemployed prolets are gone already, and if we don't catch him soon he'll clutter up the past with every wandering workingman in the country.''

"So? That's just my point,'' Koll said impatiently. "We know they've already arrived in the past; our history books say so. Now we can sit back and let this fellow distribute our refuse all over the past.''

Spanner swivelled around and confronted Quellen. "What do you think?'' he demanded. "Should we round up this fellow and stop the departure of the Hoppers? Or should we do as Koll says, and let everything go on?''

"I'll need time to study the case,'' Quellen said suspiciously. The last thing he wanted to do was be forced into making a judgment in favor of one superior over another.

"I have an idea,'' Spanner said to Koll. "Why not catch this slyster and get him to turn over his time-travel gadget to the government? Then *we* could run a government service and charge the hoppers a fee to be sent back. It's fine all around—we'd catch our man, the government would have time-travel on a platter, the hoppers would still go back without changing the past, and we'll make a little money on the deal."

Koll brightened. "Perfect solution," he said. "Brilliant, Spanner. Quellen—"

Quellen stiffened. "Yes, sir?"

"Get on it, fast. Track down this fellow and put him away, but not before you get his secret out of him. As soon as you locate him the government can go into the hopper-exporting trade."

CHAPTER II

ONCE HE was back in his own office, behind his own small but private desk, Quellen could feel important again. He rang for Brogg and Mikken, and the two UnderSecs appeared almost instantly.

"Good to see you again," Brogg said sourly. Quellen opened the vent and let oxy flow into the office, trying to capture the patronizing look Koll had flashed while doing the same thing ten minutes before.

Mikken nodded curtly. Quellen surveyed the two of them. Brogg was the one who knew the secret; a third of Quellen's salary paid him to keep quiet about Quellen's second, secret home. Big Mikken did not know and did not care; he took his orders directly from Brogg, not from Quellen.

"I suppose you're familiar with the recent prolet disappearances," Quellen began.

Brogg produced a thick stack of minislips. "As a matter of fact, I was just going to get in touch with you about them. It seems that four thousand unemployed prolets have vanished so far this year."

"What have you done so far towards solving the case?" asked Quellen.

"Well," Brogg said, pacing up and down the little

room and wiping the sweat from his heavy jowls, "I've determined that these disappearances are directly connected to historical records of the appearance of the hoppers in the late Twentieth Century and succeeding years." Brogg pointed to the book lying on Quellen's desk. "History book. I put it there for you. It confirms my findings."

Quellen ran a finger along his jawline and wondered what it was like to carry around as much fat on one's face as Brogg did. Brogg was perspiring heavily, and his face was virtually begging Quellen to open the oxy vent wider. The moment of superiority pleased the CrimeSec, and he made no move toward the wall.

"I've already taken these factors into consideration," said Quellen. "I've developed a course of action."

"Have you checked it with Koll and Spanner?" Brogg said insolently. His jowls quivered as his voice rumbled through them.

"I have," Quellen said with as much force as he could muster, angry that Brogg had so easily deflated him. "I want you to track down the slyster who's shipping these hoppers back. Bring him here. I want him caught before he sends anyone else into the past."

"Yes sir," Brogg said resignedly. "Come on, Mikken." The other assistant reluctantly left his chair and followed Brogg out. Quellen watched them quizzically through his view-window as they appeared on the street, jostled their way to a belt, and disappeared among the multitudes that thronged the streets. Then, with almost savage joy, he flipped the oxy vent to its widest, and leaned back.

After a while Quellen decided to brief himself on the situation. Conquering his apathy was not easy, since foremost in his mind was the desire to get out of Appalachia and back to Africa as quickly as he could.

He snapped on the projector and the history book began to unroll. He watched it stream by.

The first sign of invasion from the future came about 1962, when several men in strange costumes appeared in the part of Appalachia then known as Manhattan. Records show they appeared with increasing frequency throughout the next decade, and when interrogated all admitted that they had come from the future. Pressure of repeated evidence eventually forced the people of the 20th Century to the conclusion that they were actually being subjected to a peaceful but annoying invasion by time-travellers.

There was more, a whole reel more, but Quellen had had enough. He cut the projector off. The heat of the little room was oppressive, despite the air conditioning and the oxy vent. Quellen looked despairingly at the confining walls, and thought with longing of the murky stream that ran by his African retreat's front porch.

"I've done all I can," he said, and stepped out the window to catch the nearest quickboat back to his Class Thirteen apartment. Fleetingly he considered the idea of getting Brogg to handle the whole case while he went back to Africa, but he decided that would be inviting disaster.

Quellen had neglected to keep his foodstocks in good supply, he discovered, and, since his stay in

Appalachia threatened to be long or possibly permanent, he decided to replenish his stores. He fastened the *Privacy* radion to his door again and headed down the twisting flyramp to the supply shop, intending to stock up for a long siege.

As he made his way down, he noticed a sallow-looking man heading in the opposite direction up the ramp. Quellen did not recognize him, but that was unsurprising; in the crowded turmoil of Appalachia, one never got to know very many people, just the keeper of the supply shop and a handful of neighbors.

The sallow-looking man stared curiously at him and seemed to be saying something with his eyes. He brushed against Quellen and shoved a wadded minislip into his hand. Quellen unfolded it after the other had disappeared up the flyramp, and read it.

Out of work? See Lanoy. That was all it said. Instantly Quellen's CrimeSec facet came into play. Like most law-breakers in public office, he was vigorous in prosecution of other law-breakers, and there was something in Lanoy's handbill that smacked of illegality. Quellen turned with the thought of pursuing the hastily-retreating sallow man, but the other had disappeared. He could have gone almost anywhere after leaving the flyramp. *Out of work? See Lanoy.* Quellen wondered who Lanoy was and what his magic remedy was. He made up his mind that he would have Brogg look into the matter.

Carefully stowing the minislip in his pocket, Quellen entered the supply shop. The red-faced little man who ran it greeted Quellen with an unusual display of heartiness.

"Oh, it's the CrimeSec! We haven't been honored by you in a long time, CrimeSec," the rotund shopkeeper said. "I was beginning to think you'd moved. But that's impossible, isn't it? You'd have notified me if you'd gotten a promotion."

"Yes, Greevy, that's true. I've just not been around lately. Very busy these days." Quellen frowned. He didn't want the news of his absence noised all around the community. He made his order, statted the supplies upstairs, and left the supply shop.

He stepped out into the street for a moment and stood watching as the multitudes streamed past. Their clothes were of all designs and colors. They talked incessantly. The world was a beehive, vastly overpopulated and getting more so daily. Quellen longed for the quiet retreat he had built at such great cost and with so much trepidation. The more he saw of crocodiles, the less he cared for the company of the mobs who swarmed the crowded cities.

All sorts of illegal things went on—not, as in Quellen's case, justifiable efforts to escape an intolerable existence, but shady, vicious, unpardonable things. Like this Lanoy, Quellen thought, fingering the minislip in his pocket. How did he manage to hide his activities, whatever they were, from his roommates? Surely he wasn't Class Thirteen.

Quellen felt a strange kinship with the unseen Lanoy. He too, was beating the game. He was a wily one, possibly worth knowing. Then Quellen moved on.

CHAPTER III

BROGG phoned him and got him back to the office in a hurry. Quellen found his two UnderSecs waiting with a third man, a tall, angular, shabbily-dressed fellow with a broken nose that projected beaklike from his face. Brogg had turned the oxy vent up to full.

"Is this the fellow?" Quellen said. It didn't seem likely that this seedy prolet—too poor, apparently, to afford a plastic job on his nose—was the force behind the hoppers.

"Depends on what fellow you mean," Brogg said. "Tell the CrimeSec who you are," he said, nudging the prolet roughly with his elbow.

"Name is Brand," the prolet said in a thin, oddly high voice. "Class Four. I didn't mean no harm, sir—it was just that he promised me a home all my own, and a job, and fresh air—"

Brogg cut him off. "We ran up against this fellow in a drinker. He had had one or two too many and was telling everyone that he'd have a job soon."

"That's what the fellow said," Brand mumbled. "Just had to give him two hundred credits and he'd send me somewhere where everyone had a job. And I'd be able to send money back to bring my family

98

along. It sounded so good, sir.''

"What was this fellow's name?" Quellen asked sharply.

"Lanoy, sir.'' Quellen felt a startled pang of recognition at hearing the name. "Someone gave me this and told me to get in touch with him.''

Brand held out a crumpled minislip. Quellen unfolded it and read it. *"Out of work? See Lanoy."* Very interesting. He reached into his own pocket and pulled out the slip he had been handed on the flyramp. *Out of work? See Lanoy.* They were identical.

"Lanoy's sent a lot of my friends there," Brand said. "He told me they were all working and happy there, sir—"

"Where does he send them?" Quellen asked gently.

"I don't know, sir. Lanoy said he was going to tell me when I gave him the two hundred credits. I drew out all my savings. I was on my way to him, and I just dropped in for a short one—when—when—"

"When we found him," Brogg finished. "Telling everyone in sight that he was heading to Lanoy to get a job.''

"Hmm. Do you know what the hoppers are, Brand?''

"No, sir.''

"Never mind, then. Suppose you take us to Lanoy.''

"I can't do that. It wouldn't be fair. All my friends—"

"Suppose we *make* you take us to Lanoy," Quellen said.

"But he was going to give me a job! I can't do it. Please, sir."

Brogg looked at Quellen. "Let me try," he said. "Lanoy was going to give you a job, you say? For two hundred credits?"

"Yes, sir."

"Suppose we tell you that we'll give you a job for nothing. No charge at all, just lead us to Lanoy and we'll send you where he was going to send you, only free. And we'll send your family along too."

Quellen smiled. Brogg was a much better psychologist than he was; he was forced to admit.

"That's fair," Brand said. "I'll take you. I feel bad about it—Lanoy was nice to me—but if you say you'll send me for nix . . ."

"Quite right, Brand," Brogg said.

"I'll do it, then."

Quellen turned down the oxy vent. "Let's go before he changes his mind," Brogg gestured to Mikken, who led Brand out.

"Are you coming with us, sir?" Brogg asked. There was just a hint of sarcasm behind Brogg's obsequious tones. "It'll probably be a pretty filthy part of town."

Quellen shivered. "You're right," he said. "You two take him. I'll wait here."

As soon as they were gone, Quellen rang Koll.

"We're hot on the trail," he said. "Brogg and Mikken have found the man who's doing it, and they'll bring him back."

"Fine work," Koll said coldly. "It should be an interesting investigation. But please don't disturb us for a while. Spanner and I are discussing departmental status changes." He hung up.

Now what did that mean? Quellen wondered. By now he was sure Koll knew about Africa. Brogg had probably been offered a bigger bribe to talk than Quellen had given him to be silent, and he had sold out to the highest bidder. Of course, Koll might have meant a promotion, but demotion was a more likely change in status to discuss.

Quellen's offense was a unique one. No one else, to his knowledge, had been shrewd enough to find a way out of heavily-overpopulated Appalachia, the octopus of a city that spread all over the eastern half of North America. Of all the two hundred million inhabitants of Appalachia, only Joseph Quellen CrimeSec had been clever enough to find a bit of unknown and unsettled land in the heart of Africa and build himself a second home there. He had the standard Class Thirteen cubicle in Appalachia, plus a Class Twenty mansion beyond the dreams of most mortals, beside a murky stream in the Congo. It was nice, very nice, for a man whose soul rebelled at the insect-like existence in Appalachia.

The only trouble was that it took money to keep people bribed. There were a few who had to know that Quellen was living luxuriously in Africa instead of dwelling in a ten-by-ten cubicle in Northwest Appalachia, like a good Thirteen. Someone—Brogg, he was sure—had sold out to Koll. And Quellen was on thin ice indeed.

A demotion would rob him even of the privilege of maintaining a private cubicle, and he would go back to sharing his home, as he had with unlamented Marok. It hadn't been so bad when he had been below Class Twelve and lived, first in the dorms, then in gradually more private rooms. He hadn't minded other people so much when he was younger. But then to move to Class Twelve and be put into a room with just one other person, that had been the most painful of all, souring Quellen permanently.

Marok had been a genuinely fine fellow, Quellen reflected. But he had jarred on Quellen's nerves, with his sloppiness and his unending visiphone calls and his constant presence. Quellen had longed for the day when he would reach Thirteen and live alone, no longer with a roommate as a constant check. He would be free—free to hide from the crowd.

Did Koll know? He'd soon find out whether he did.

The phone clicked. It was Brogg.

"We have him," Brogg said. "We're on our way back."

"Fine work, fine work."

Quellen dialed Koll. "We've caught the man," he said. "Brogg and Mikken are bringing him back here for interrogation."

"Good job," Koll said, and Quellen noted the trace of an honest smile flickering on the small man's lips. "I've just filled out a promotion form for you, by the way," he added casually. "It seems unfair to let the CrimeSec live in a Class Thirteen unit when he rates at least a Fourteen."

So he doesn't know after all, Quellen thought. Then another thought came: how could he move the illegal stat to new quarters without being detected? Perhaps Koll was only leading him deeper into a trap. Quellen pressed his palms against his temples and shivered, waiting, for Brogg, Mikken—and Lanoy.

"You admit you've been sending people into the past?" Quellen demanded.

"Sure," said the little man flippantly. Quellen watched him and felt an irrational pulse of anger go through him. "Sure. I'll send you back for two hundred creds."

Brogg stood with folded arms behind the little man, and Quellen faced him over the table.

"You're Lanoy?"

"That's my name." He was a small, dark, intense, rabbity sort of man, with thin lips constantly moving. "Sure, I'm Lanoy." The little man radiated a confident warmth. He sat with his legs crossed and his head thrown back.

"It was pretty nasty the way your boys tracked me down," Lanoy said. "It was bad enough that you fooled that poor prolet into leading you to me, but they didn't need to rough me up. I'm not doing anything illegal, you know. I ought to sue."

"You're disturbing the past thousand years!"

"I am not," Lanoy said calmly. "They've already been disturbed. I'm just seeing to it that past history takes place the way it took place, if you know what I mean."

Quellen stood up, but found he had no room to move in the tiny office, and sat down again ineffectually. He felt strangely weak in the presence of the slyster.

"But you're sending prolets back to become the hoppers. Why?"

Lanoy smiled. "To earn a living. Surely you understand that. I'm in possession of a very valuable process, and I want to make sure I get all I can out of it."

"Did you invent time-travel?"

"It doesn't matter," said Lanoy. "I control it."

"Why don't you simply go back in time and steal or place bets to make a living?"

"I could," Lanoy admitted. "But the process is irreversible, and there's no way of getting back to the present again. And I like it here, thank you."

"Look, Lanoy," Quellen said. "I'll be frank: we want your time-travel gimmick, and we want it fast."

"Sorry," said Lanoy. "Private property. You don't have any right to it."

Quellen thought of Koll and Spanner, and got angry and frightened at the same time. "When I get through with you you'll wish you'd used your own machine and gone back a million years."

Lanoy remained calm, and Quellen was surprised to see Brogg smiling. "Come now, CrimeSec," the slyster said. "You're starting to get angry, and that's always illogical."

Quellen saw the truth of what Lanoy was saying, but he lost the struggle to calm himself. "I'll keep you under arrest until you rot," he threatened.

"Now where will that get you?" Lanoy asked. "Would you mind giving me a little more oxy in here, please, by the way? I'm suffocating."

In his astonishment Quellen opened the vent wide. Brogg registered surprise, and even Mikken blinked at Lanoy's breach of taste.

"If you arrest me I'll break you, Quellen. There's nothing illegal in what I'm doing. Look here—I'm a registered slyster." Lanoy produced a card, properly stamped.

Quellen didn't know what to say. Lanoy definitely had him on the run, he knew, and Brogg was enjoying his discomfiture immensely. Quellen chewed his lip, watching the little man closely, and wishing fervently that he were back beside his Congo stream throwing rocks at the crocodiles.

"I'm going to put a stop to your time-travelling, anyway," Quellen finally said.

Lanoy chuckled. "I wouldn't advise it, Quellen."

"CrimeSec to you, Lanoy."

"I wouldn't advise it, *Quellen*," Lanoy repeated. "If you cut off the hoppers now, you'll turn the past topsy-turvy. Those people went back. It's recorded in history. Some of them married and had children, and the descendants of those children are alive today. For all you know, Quellen, you may be the descendant of a hopper I'm going to send back next week—and if that hopper never gets back, Quellen, you'll pop out of existence like a snuffed candle. Sound like a pleasant way to die, CrimeSec?"

Quellen stared glumly. Brogg stood silently behind Lanoy, and it became apparent to the CrimeSec now that the burly UnderSec had been gunning for Quellen's job all along, and that Lanoy was doing an effective job of eliminating the last stumbling-block in his way. Marok, Koll, Spanner, Brogg, and now Lanoy—they were all determined to see Quellen enmeshed. It was an unvoiced conspiracy. Silently he cursed the two hundred million jostling inhabitants of Appalachia, and wondered if he'd every know a moment's solitude again.

"The past won't be changed, Lanoy," he said. "We'll lock you up, all right, and take away your machine, but we'll see to it ourselves that the hoppers go back. We're no fools, Lanoy. We'll see to it that everything stays as it is."

Lanoy watched him almost with pity for a moment, as one might observe a particularly rare butterfly impaled on a mounting board.

"Is that your game, CrimeSec? Why didn't you tell me that before? In that case I'll have to take steps to protect myself."

Quellen felt like hiding. "What are you going to do?"

"Suppose we talk it over privately, Quellen," the slyster said. "I might say some things you wouldn't want your subordinates to hear."

Quellen glanced at Brogg. "Have you searched him?"

"He's clean," Brogg said. "Nothing to fear. We'll wait in the anteroom. Come on, Mikken."

Ponderously, Brogg stalked out of the room, followed by the silent Mikken.

With the occupants of the room numbering just two, Quellen moved to cut down the oxy vent.

"Leave it up, Quellen," Lanoy said. "I like to breathe well at government expense."

"What's your game?" Quellen asked. He was angry; Lanoy was a completely vicious creature who offended Quellen's pride and dignity.

"I'll be blunt with you, CrimeSec," the slyster said. "I want my freedom, and I want to continue in business. I like it that way. That's what I want. You want to arrest me and take over my business. That's what you want. Right?"

"Yes."

"Now in a situation like that we have an interplay of mutually exclusive desires. So the stronger of the two forces wins—all the time. I'm stronger, and so you'll have to let me go and forget all about the investigation."

"Who says you're stronger, Lanoy?"

"I'm strong because you're weak. I know a lot of things about you, Quellen. I know how you hate crowds and like fresh air and open spaces. These are pretty awkward idiosyncrasies to live with in a world like ours, aren't they?"

"Go on," said Quellen. He cursed Brogg silently—no one else could have revealed his secret to Lanoy.

"So you're going to let me walk out of here, or else you'll find yourself back in a Class Twelve or Ten unit. You won't like it much there, CrimeSec. You'll have to share a room and you may not like your room-mate, but there'll be nothing you can do. And when you have a room-mate, you won't be free to run away. He'll report you."

"What do you mean, run away?" Quellen's voice was little more than a husky whisper.

"I mean run away to Africa, Quellen."

That was it, Quellen thought. Now it's over; Brogg's sold me down the river. With Lanoy in possession of Quellen's secret, Quellen was completely in the little slyster's power.

"I hate to do this to you, Quellen. You're a pretty good sort, caught in a world you didn't make and don't especially like. But it's either you or me, and you know who always wins in deals like that."

Check and mate.

"Go ahead," Quellen whispered. "Get moving."

"I knew you'd see it my way," Lanoy said. "I'll leave now. You don't interfere with me, and Koll won't ever know about your little shack."

"Get out," Quellen said.

Lanoy got up, saluted Quellen, and slipped out through the door.

CHAPTER IV

AS LANOY left, Koll entered. Quellen, his face in his hands, saw Koll out of the corner of one eye and thought for a moment that it was Lanoy returning. Then he looked up.

"I thought I'd have a look at your slyster," Koll said. "But I see he's not around."

"I sent him inside," Quellen said weakly.

"I'll check," said Koll. "I'm quite curious about him." He left, and Brogg entered.

"Have a nice chat, CrimeSec?" Brogg asked, smiling. As always, the fat man's forehead was strung with a row of perspiration-beads.

"Very nice, thank you." Quellen looked imploringly at his assistant. If only he could be left alone for a few moments!

"He doesn't seem to be here any more, CrimeSec. I had a few questions for your friend Lanoy, but I can't find him."

"I don't know where he went to, Brogg."

"Are you sure, now, CrimeSec? Where is he, Quellen?" he said maliciously.

"I don't know." It was the first time Brogg had dropped the honorific in addressing Quellen. "Go away."

Brogg smiled slyly and left, closing the door with care. Quellen sat in his pneumochair, shaking his head from side to side. He was in for it now. If he failed to produce Lanoy, they'd have his neck. If he recaptured the little slyster, Lanoy would give the show away. Either way they had him.

He tiptoed through the front office, where Brogg glared at him with evident interest, stepped out into the crowded street and caught the first quickboat back to his apartment. It was good to be alone again. He wandered around aimlessly for a moment, and then walked over to face the stat.

All he had to do was step through it and he'd be back in Africa, by the side of the twisting stream and the crocodiles. No more job, but they'd never find him, and he could spend the rest of his days peacefully.

No good, he thought dismally. It wasn't safe, with Brogg and Lanoy knowing. Between the two of them, they'd ferret him out quickly enough. Africa held no security.

Besides, he felt a strange new feeling growing in him—a feeling that he was put upon, that he was a sort of martyr to overcrowding. He thrust his hands in his pockets and stood before the stat, revolving in his mind the implications of this new concept. A world he never made, Lanoy had said.

All guilt dissolved. Let Koll unravel the mess to suit himself, Quellen thought.

It was done.

There was a swirling and a twisting and Quellen felt as if he had been turned inside-out and disembowelled. He was floating on a purple cloud high above some indistinct terrain, and he was falling. He dropped, heels over head, and landed in a scrambled heap on a long green carpet. He lay there for a moment or two, just holding on to the ground.

A handful of the carpet tore off in his fist. He looked at it with a puzzled expression on his face.

Grass.

The clean smell of the air hit him next, almost as a physical shock. It smelled like a room with full oxy, but this was outdoors.

Quellen gathered himself together and stood up. The grassy carpet extended in all directions, and in front of him there was a great thicket of trees.

He had seen trees in Africa. There were none in Appalachia. He looked. A small gray bird came out on the overhanging branch of the nearest tree and began to chirp, unafraid, at Quellen. He smiled.

He wondered how long Koll and Brogg would search for him, and whether Brogg could cope with Lanoy. He hoped not; Brogg was a scoundrel, and Lanoy, despite his slyster habits, was a gentleman.

Quellen began to move toward the forest. He would have to locate a stream and build a house next to it, he decided. He could make the house as big as he wanted.

He felt no guilt. He had been a misfit, thrown into a world he could only hate and which could only ensnarl him. Now he had his chance; it was all up to him.

Two deer came bounding out of the forest. Quellen stood aghast. He had never seen animals that size. Happily, they skipped off into the distance.

Quellen's heart began to sing as he filled his lungs with the sweet air. Marok, Koll, Spanner, Brogg.

They began to fade and blur. Good old Lanoy, he thought. He'd kept his word after all.

The world is mine, Quellen thought. So now I'm a hopper, too—taking the longest hop of all.

A tall, red-skinned man emerged from the forest and stood near a tree, regarding Quellen gravely. He was dressed in a leather belt, a pair of sandals, and nothing else, and in his hair was a decorative feather. The red-skinned man studied Quellen for a moment and then raised his arm in a gesture Quellen could not fail to interpret. A warm feeling of comradeship glowed in Quellen.

Smiling at last, Quellen went forward to meet him, palm upraised.

BLAZE OF GLORY

THEY LIST John Murchison as one of the great heroes of space—a brave man and true, who willingly sacrificed himself to save his ship. He won his immortality on the way back from Shaula II.

One thing's wrong, though. He was brave, but he wasn't willing. He wasn't the self-sacrificing type. I'm inclined to think it was murder—or maybe execution—by remote control, you might say.

I guess they pick spaceship crews at random, probably by yanking a handful of cards from the big computer and throwing them up at the BuSpace roof. The ones that stick get picked. At least, that's the only way a man like Murchison could have been sent to Shaula II in the first place.

Murchison was tall, bull-necked, coarse-featured, hard-swearing, a spaceman of a type that had never existed except in storytapes for the very young—the only kind Murchison was likely to have studied. He was our chief signal officer.

Somewhere, he had picked up an awesome technical competence; he could handle any sort of communication device with supernatural ease. I once saw him tinker with a complex little Caphian artifact

112

that had been buried for half a million years and have it detecting the 21-centimeter "hydrogen song" within minutes. How he knew the little widget was a star-mapping device, I will never understand.

But coupled with Murchison's extraordinary special skill was an irascibility, flaring into seemingly unmotivated anger at unpredictable times, that made him a prime risk on a planet like Shaula II. There was something wrong with his emotional circuit-breaker, you could never tell when he'd overload, start fizzing and sparking, and blow off a couple of megawatts of temper.

You must admit this is not the ideal sort of man to send to a world whose inhabitants are listed in the Extraterrestrial Catalogue as *"wise, somewhat world-weary, exceedingly gentle, non-aggressive to an extreme degree and thus subject to exploitation. The Shaulans must be handled with great patience and forbearance, and should be given the respect due one of the Galaxy's elder races."*

I had never been to Shaula II, but I had a sharp mental image of the Shaulans: melancholy old men, pondering the whichness of the why, whom the first loud shout would drop in their tracks. So it caught me by surprise when the time came to affix my hancock to the roster of the *Felicific* and I saw on the line above mine the scribbled words *Murchison, John F., Chief, Signal Officer.*

I signed my name—*Loeb, Ernest T., Second Officer*—picked up my pay voucher and walked away somewhat dizzily. I was thinking of the time I had seen Murchison, John F., giving a Denebolan frogman the beating of his life, for no particular reason at all.

"All the rain here makes me sick," was all Murchison cared to say; the frogman lived and Big Jawn got an X on his psych report.

Now he was shipping out for Shaula? Well, maybe so—but my faith in the computer that makes up spaceship complements was seriously shaken.

Ours was the fourth or fifth expedition to Shaula II. The planet—second of seven in orbit around the brighest star in Scorpio's tail—was small and scrubby, but of great strategic importance as a lookout spot for that sector of the Galaxy. The natives hadn't minded our intrusion and so a military base had been established there with no preliminary haggling whatever.

The *Felicific* was a standard warp-conversion-drive ship holding thirty-six men. It had the usual crew of eight, plus a cargo of twenty-eight of Terra's finest, being sent out as replacements for the current staff of the base.

We blasted on 3 July 2530, a warmish day, made the conversion from ion-drive to warp-drive as soon as we were clear of the Solar System, and popped back into normal space three weeks later and two hundred light-years away. It was a routine trip in all respects.

With the warp-conversion drive, a ship is equipped to travel both long distances and short. It handles the long hops via subspace warp, and the short ones by good old standard ion-drive seat-of-the-spacesuit navigating. It's a good setup and the extra mass that the double drive requires is more than compensated for by the saving in time and maneuverability.

The warp-drive part of the trip was pre-plotted and just about pre-traveled for us; no headaches *there*.

But when we blurped back into the continuum about half a light-year from Shaula, the human factor entered the situation. Meaning Murchison, of course.

It was his job to check and tend the network of telemetering systems that acted as the ship's eyes, to make sure the mass-detectors were operating, to smooth the bugs out of the communications channels between navigator and captain and drive-deck. In brief, he was the man who made it possible for us to land.

Every ship carried a spare signalman, just in case. In normal circumstances, the spare never got much work. When the time came for the landing, Captain Knight buzzed me and told me to start lining up the men who would take part. Naturally, I signaled Murchison first—he was our chief signal officer.

His voice was a slow rasping drawl, "Yeah?"

"Second Officer Loeb. Prepare for landing, double-fast. Navigator Henrichs has the chart set up for you and he's waiting for your call."

There was a pause. Then: "I don't feel like it, Loeb."

I shut my eyes, held my breath and counted to three by fractions. Then I said, "Would you mind repeating that, Mr. Murchison?"

"Hell, Loeb, I'm fixing something. Why do you want to land now?"

"I don't make up the schedules," I said.

"Then who in blazes does? Tell him I'm busy!"

I turned down my phone's volume.

"Busy doing what?"

"Busy doing nothing. Get off the line and I'll call Henrichs."

I grunted and broke contact. He'd just been ragging me. Once again, Murchison had been ornery for the sheer sake of being ornery. One of these days, he was going to refuse to handle the landing entirely. And that day, I told myself, is the day we'll crate him up and shove him through the disposal lock.

Murchison had his skills and he applied them—when he felt like it. But only if he believed that he would profit. He never did anything unwillingly, because if he couldn't find it in himself to do it willingly, he wouldn't do it at all. It was impossible to *make* him do something.

Unwisely, we tolerated it. But someday he would get a captain who didn't understand him and he'd be slapped with a sentence of mutiny. For his sake, I hoped not. The penalty for mutiny in space is the same as it always has been—death.

With Murchison's cooperation gratefully accepted, we targeted on Shaula II, which was then at perihelion, and orbited in. Down in his little cubicle, Murchison worked like a demon, taking charge of the ships' landing system in a tremendous way. He was a fantastic signalman when he wanted to be.

Later that day, the spinning red ball that was Shaula II hung just ahead of us, close enough to let us see the three blobs of continents and the big, choppy hydrocarbon ocean that licked them smooth.

The Terran base on Continent Three beamed us a landing guide. Murchison picked it up, fed it through the computer bank to Navigator Henrichs and we homed in for the landing.

The Terran base consisted of a couple of blockhouses, a sprawling barracks and a good-sized radar parabola, all set in a ring out on an almost mathematically flat plain. Shaula II was a great world for plains; Columbus would have had the devil's time convincing people *this* world was round!

Murchison guided us to a glassy-looking area not far from the base and we touched down. The *Felicific* creaked and groaned a little as the landing-jacks absorbed its weight. Green lights went on all over the ship. We were free to go outside.

A welcoming committee was on hand out there: eight members of the base staff, clad in shorts and topees. Regulation uniforms went by the board on oven-hot Shaula II. The eight looked awfully happy to see us.

Coming over the flat sandy plain from the base were a dozen or so others, running, and behind them I could see even more. They were understandably glad we were here. Twenty-eight of them had spent a full year on Shaula II; they were eligible for their parity-program year's vacation.

There were some other—things—moving toward us. They came slowly, with grace and dignity. I had expected to be impressed with the Shaulans and I was.

They were erect bipeds about four feet tall, with long thin arms dangling to their knees. Their gray skins were grainy and rough, and their dark eyes—they had three, arranged triangularly—were deep-set and brooding. A fleshy sort of cowl or cobra-hood curled up from their necks to shield their round hairless skulls. The aliens were six in number and even the youngest-looking of them seemed ancient.

A brown-faced young man wearing shorts, topee and tattooed stars stepped forward and said, "I'm General Gloster. I'm in charge here."

117

The captain acknowledged his greeting. "Knight of the *Felicific*. We have your relief men with us."

"I sure as hell hope you do," Gloster said. "Be kind of silly to come all this way without them."

We all laughed a little over that. By now, we were ringed in by at least fifty Earthmen, probably the entire base complement—we didn't rotate the entire base staff at once, of course—and the six aliens.

The twenty-eight youngsters we had ferried here were looking around the place curiously, apprehensive about this hot, dry, flat planet that would be their home for the next sidereal year.

The crew of the *Felicific* had gathered in a little knot near the ship. Most of them probably felt the way I did—glad we'd be on our way home in a couple of days.

Murchison was squinting at the six aliens. I wondered what he was thinking about.

The bunch of us traipsed back the half mile or so to the settlement. Gloster walked with Knight and myself, prattling volubly about the progress the base was making, and the twenty-eight newcomers mingled with the twenty-eight who were being relieved. Murchison walked by himself, kicking up puffs of red dust and glowering in his usual manner. The six aliens accompanied us at some distance.

"We keep building all the time," Gloster explained when we were within the compound. "Branching out, setting up new equipment, erecting new quarters, shoring up the old stuff. That radar parabola out there wasn't up last replacement trip."

I looked around. "The place looks fine, General." It was strange calling a man half my age *General*, but the Service sometimes works that way. "When do you plan to set up your telescope?''

"Next year, maybe." He glanced out the window at the featureless landscape. "We keep building all the time. Got to make something out of this planet. We're doing a damn fine job—never recognize the place in a couple of years."

"How about the natives?" the captain asked. "You have much contact with them?"

Gloster shrugged. "As much as they'll allow. They're a proud old race—only a handful of them left. But what a race they must have been once!"

I found Gloster's boyish enthusiasm discomforting. "Do you think we could meet one of the aliens before we go?" I asked.

"I'll see about it." Gloster picked up a phone. "McHenry? There any natives in the compound now? Good. Send him up, will you?"

Moments later, one of the shorts-clad men appeared, hand in hand with an alien. At close range, the Shaulan looked almost frighteningly old. A maze of wrinkles gullied its noseless face, running from the triple eyes down to the dots of nostrils to the sagging, heavy-lipped mouth.

"This is Azga," Gloster said. "Azga, meet Captain Knight and Second Officer Loeb of the *Felicific*."

The creature offered a wobbly sort of bow and said in a deep, resonant, almost human croak, "I am very humble indeed in your presence, Captain Knight and Second Officer Loeb."

Azga straightened painfully from bowing and the three eyes fixed on mine. I felt like squirming, but I stared back. It was like looking into a mirror that gave the wrong reflection.

Yet there was something calm and wise and good about the grotesque creature, something relaxing and terribly fragile. The rough gray skin looked like precious leather, and the hood over the skull appeared to shield it from worry and harm. A faint musty odor wandered through the room.

We looked at each other—Knight and Gloster and McHenry and I—and we remained silent. Now that the Shaulan was here, what could we say? What *new* thing could we possibly tell the ancient creature?

I was fumbling for words to express my feeling when the sharp buzz of the phone cut across the uncomfortable silence.

Gloster nodded curtly to McHenry, who answered. The man listened for a moment. "Captain Knight, it's for you."

Puzzled, Knight took the receiver. He held it long enough to hear about three sentences and turned to me. "Loeb, commandeer a landcar from someone in the compound and get back to the ship. Murchison's tangling with one of the aliens."

I hotfooted down into the compound and spotted an enlisted man tooling up his landcar. I pulled rank and requisitioned it, and minutes later I was parking it outside the *Felicific* and was clambering up the catwalk.

An excited-looking recruit stood at the open airlock.

"Where's Murchison?" I asked.

"Down in the communicator cabin, sir. He's got an alien in there with him. There's gonna be trouble."

I remembered Denebola and Murchison kicking the stuffings out of a groaning frogman. I groaned a little myself and dashed down the companionway.

The communications cabin was Murchison's inner sanctum, a cubicle off the astro deck where he worked and kept control over the *Felicific's* communications network.

I yanked open the door and saw him at the far end of the cabin, holding a massive crescent wrench and glaring at a Shaulan facing him. The Shaulan had its back to me. It looked small and squat and helpless.

Murchison saw me as I entered. "Get out of here, Loeb. This isn't your affair."

"What's going on here?" I snapped.

"This alien snooping around. I'm gonna let him have it with the wrench."

"I meant no harm," the alien boomed sadly. "Mere philosophical interest in your strange machines, nothing more. If I have offended a folkway of yours, I humbly apologize. It is not the way of my people to give offense."

I walked forward and took a position between them, making sure I wasn't within easy reach of Murchison's wrench. He was standing there with his nostrils spread, his eyes cold and hard, his breath pumping noisily. He was angry, and an angry Murchison was a frightening sight.

He took two heavy steps toward me. "I told you to get out. This is my cabin, Loeb. And neither you nor any aliens got any business in it."

"Put down that wrench, Murchison. It's an order."

He laughed contemptuously. "Signal officers don't have to take orders from anyone but the captain if they think the safety of the ship is jeopardized. And I do. There's a dangerous alien in here."

"Be reasonable," I said. "This Shaulan's not dangerous. He only wanted to look around. Just curious."

The wrench wiggled warningly. I wished I had a blaster with me, but I hadn't thought of bringing a weapon. The alien faced Murchison quite calmly, as if confident the signalman would never strike anything so old and delicate.

"You'd better leave," I said to the alien.

"No!" Murchison roared. He shoved me to one side and went after the Shaulan.

The alien stood there, waiting, as Murchison came on. I tried to drag the big man away, but there was no stopping him.

At least he didn't use the wrench. He let it slip clangingly to the floor and slapped the alien open-handed across its face. The Shaulan backed up a few feet. A trickle of bluish fluid worked its way along its mouth.

Murchison raised his hand again. "Damned snooper! I'll teach you to poke in my cabin!" He hit the alien again.

This time the Shaulan folded up accordionwise and huddled on the floor. It focused those three deep solid-black eyes on Muchison reproachfully.

Murchison looked back. They stared at each other for a long moment, until it seemed that their eyes were linked by an invisible cord. Then Murchison looked away.

"Get out of here," he muttered.

The Shaulan rose and departed, limping a little, but still intact. Those aliens were more solid than they seemed.

"I guess you're going to put me in the brig," Murchison said to me. "Okay, I'll go quietly."

We didn't brig him, because there was nothing to be gained by that. He got the silent treatment instead. The men at the base would have nothing to do with him whatsoever because, in their year on Shaula, they had developed a respect for the aliens not far from worship, and any man who would actually use physical violence—well, he just wasn't worth wasting breath on.

The men of our crew gave him a wide berth, too. He wandered among us, a tall, powerful figure with anger and loneliness stamped on his face, and he said nothing to any of us and no one said anything to him. Whenever he saw one of the aliens, he went far out of his way to avoid a meeting.

Murchison got another X on his psych report, and that second X meant he'd never be allowed to visit any world inhabited by intelligent life again. It was a BuSpace regulation, one of the many they have for the purpose of locking the barn door too late.

Three days went by this way on Shaula. On the fourth, we took aboard the twenty-eight departing men, said good-by to Gloster and his staff and the twenty-eight we had ferried out to him, and— somewhat guiltily—good-by to the Shaulans, too.

The six of them showed up for our blastoff, including the somewhat battered one who had had the run-in with Murchison. They wished us well, gravely, without any sign of bitterness. For the hundredth time, I was astonished by their patience, their wisdom, their understanding.

I held Azga's rough hand in mine and finally managed to tell him what I had been wanting to say since our first meeting—how much I hoped we'd eventually reach the mental equilibrium and inner calm of the Shaulans. He smiled warmly at me and I said good-by and entered the ship.

We ran the usual pre-blast checkups and got ready for departure. Communications was working well—Murchison had none of his usual grumbles and complaints—and we were off the ground in record time.

A couple of days of ion-drive, three weeks of warp, two more of ion-drive deceleration, and we would be back on Earth.

The three weeks passed slowly, of course; when Earth lies ahead of you, time drags. But after the interminable grayness of warp came the sudden wrenching twist and the bright slippery *sliding* feeling as our Bohling generator threw us back into ordinary space.

I pushed down the communicator stud near my arm and heard the voice of Navigator Henrichs saying, "Murchison, give me the coordinates, will you?"

"Hold on," came Murchison's growl. "You'll get your coordinates as soon as I got 'em."

There was a pause; then Captain Knight said, "Murchison, what's holding up those coordinates? Where are we, anyway? Turn on the visiplates!"

"*Please*, Captain." Murchison's heavy voice was surprisingly polite. Then he ruined it. "Please be good enough to shut up and let a man think."

"Murchison—" Knight sputtered, and stopped.

We all knew one solid fact about our signalman: he did as he wanted. No one ever coerced him into anything.

So we waited, spinning end-over-end somewhere in the vicinity of Earth, completely blind behind our wall of metal. Until Murchison chose to feed us some data, we had no way of bringing the ship down.

Three more minutes went by. Then the private circuit Knight used when he wanted to talk to me alone lit up, and he said, "Loeb, go down to Communications and see what's holding Murchison up. We can't stay here forever."

I pocketed a blaster—I hate making mistakes more than once—and left my cabin. I walked to the companionway, turned to the left, hit the drophatch and found myself outside Murchison's door.

I knocked.

"Get away from here, Loeb!" Murchison bellowed from within.

I had forgotten that he had rigged a one-way vision circuit outside his door. I said, "Let me in, Murchison. Let me in or I'll blast out the lock."

I heard a heavy sigh and the whisper of the lock contracting. "Come on in, then."

Nervously I pushed the door open and poked my head and the blaster snout in, half expecting Murchison to leap on me from above. But he was sitting at an equipment-jammed desk, scribbling notes, which surprised me. I stood waiting for him to look up.

And finally he did. I gasped when I saw his face: drawn, harried, pale, tense. I had never seen an expression like that on Murchison's face before.

"What's going on?" I asked. "We're all waiting to get moving and—"

He turned to face me squarely. "You want to know what's going on, Loeb? Well, listen: the ship's blind. None of the equipment is reading anything. No telemeter pickup, no visual, no nothing. *You* scrape up some coordinates, if you can."

We held a little meeting half an hour later, in the ship's Common Room. Murchison was there, and Knight, and myself, and Navigator Henrichs, and three representatives of the cargo.

"How did this happen?" Knight demanded.

Murchison shrugged. "It happened while we were in warp."

Knight glanced at Henrichs. "You ever hear of such a thing happening before?" He seemed to suspect Murchison of funny business.

But Henrichs shook his head. "No, Chief. And there's a good reason why, too. If this happens to a ship, the ship doesn't get back to tell about it."

Captain Knight looked gray-faced. He asked worriedly, "What could have caused this?"

"No one knows what subspace conditions are like," Henrichs said. "It may have been a fluke magnetic field, as Murchison suggests. Or anything at all. The question's not what did it, Captain—it's how do we get back."

"Murchison, is there any chance you can repair the instruments?"

"No."

"Just like that—flat *no*? Hell, man, we've seen you do wonders with instruments on the blink before."

"No," Murchison repeated solidly. "I tried. I can't do a damned thing."

"That means we're finished, doesn't it?" asked Carney, one of our returnees. His voice was a little wild. "We might just as well have stayed on Shaula! At least we'd still be alive!"

"It looks pretty lousy," Henrichs admitted. The thin-faced navigator was frowning blackly. "We don't dare try a blind approach. There's nothing we can do. Nothing at all."

"There's one thing," Murchison said.

All eyes turned to him.

"What's that?" Knight asked.

"Put a man in a spacesuit and anchor him to the skin of the ship. Have him guide us in by voice—he'll be able to see, even if we can't."

"He'd incinerate once we hit Earth's atmosphere," I said. "We'd lose a man and still have to land blind."

Murchison puckered his thick lower lip. "You'll be able to judge the ship's height by hull temperature when you're that close. Besides, as soon as the ship's inside the ionosphere, you can use ordinary radio for the rest of the way down. The trick is to get *that* far."

"I think it's worth a try," Captain Knight said. "I guess we'll have to draw lots. Loeb, get some spaghetti from the galley to use as straws." His voice was grim.

"Never mind," Murchison said.

"How's that again?"

"I said never mind. Forget about drawing straws. I'll go."

"Murchison—"

"*Skip it!*" he barked. "It's a failure in my department, so I'm going to go out there. I volunteer, get it? If anyone else wants to, I'll wrestle him for it." He looked around at us. No one moved. "I don't hear any takers. I'll assume the job's mine." Sweat streamed down his face.

There was a startled silence, broken when Carney made the lousiest remark I've ever heard mortal man utter. "You're trying to make it up for hitting that defenseless Shaulan, eh, Murchison? Now you want to be a hero to even things up!"

But the big man only turned to Carney and said quietly, "You're just as blind as the others. You don't know how rotten those *defenseless* Shaulans are, any of you. Or what they did to us." He spat. "You all make me sick. I'm going out there."

He turned and walked away—out, to get into his spacesuit and climb onto the ship's skin.

Murchison's explicit instructions, relayed from the outside of the ship, allowed Henrichs to bring us in. It was quite a feat of teamwork.

At 50,000 feet above Earth, Murchison's voice suddenly cut out. We were able to pick up ground-to-ship radio by then and we taxied down. Later, they told us it seemed like a blazing candle riding the ship's back. A bright, clear flame flared for a moment when we cleaved the atmosphere.

And I remember the look on Murchison's face as he left us to go out there. It was tense, bitter, strained—as if he were being *compelled* to go outside—as if he had no choice about volunteering for martyrdom.

I often wonder about that now. No one had ever made Murchison do anything he didn't want to do—until then.

We think of the Shaulans as gentle, meek, defenseless. Murchison crossed one of them, and he died. Gentle, meek, yes—but defenseless?

Maybe they sabotaged the ship somehow and forced Murchison into self-martyrdom because he knew he'd been the cause. I don't know.

It sort of tarnishes his glorious halo.

But sometimes I think Murchison was right about the Shaulans, after all. In any case, I've never been back there. And I don't intend to, even if the computer picks me to go.

WARM MAN

NO ONE was ever quite sure just when Mr. Hallinan came to live in New Brewster. Lonny Dewitt, who ought to know, testified that Mr. Hallinan died on December 3, at 3:30 in the afternoon, but as for the day of his arrival no one could be nearly so precise.

It was simply that one day there was no one living in the unoccupied split-level on Melon Hill, and then the next *he* was there, seemingly having grown out of the woodwork during the night, ready and willing to spread his cheer and warmth throughout the whole of the small suburban community. Daisy Moncrieff, New Brewster's ineffable hostess, was responsible for making the first overtures toward Mr. Hallinan. It was two days after she had first observed lights in the Melon Hill place that she decided the time had come to scrutinize the newcomers, to determine their place in New Brewster society. Donning a light wrap, for it was a coolish October day, she left her house in early forenoon and went on foot down Copperbeech Road to the Melon Hill turnoff, and then climbed the sloping hill till she reached the split-level.

The name was already on the mailbox: DAVIS HALLINAN. That probably meant they'd been living there a good deal longer than just two days, thought Mrs. Moncrieff; perhaps they'd be insulted by the tardiness of the invitation? She shrugged and used the doorknocker.

A tall man in early middle age appeared, smiling benignly. Mrs. Moncrieff was thus the first recipient of the uncanny warmth that Davis Halliman was to radiate throughout New Brewster before his strange death. His eyes were deep and solemn, with warm lights shining in them; his hair was a dignified gray-white mane.

"Good morning. I'm Mrs. Moncrieff—*Daisy* Moncrieff, from the big house down on Copperbeech Road. You must be Mr. Hallinan. May I come in?"

"Ah—please, no, Mrs. Moncrieff. The place is still a chaos. Would you mind staying on the porch?"

He closed the door behind him—Mrs. Moncrieff later claimed that she had a fleeting view of the interior and saw unpainted walls and dust-covered bare floors—and drew one of the rusty porch chairs for her.

"Is your wife at home, Mr. Hallinan?"

"There's just me, I'm afraid. I live alone."

"Oh." Mrs. Moncrieff, discomforted, managed a grin none the less. In New Brewster *everyone* was married; the idea of a bachelor or a widower coming to settle there was strange, disconcerting . . . and just a little pleasant, she added, surprised at herself.

"My purpose in coming was to invite you to meet some of your new neighbors tonight—if you're free, that is. I'm having a cocktail party at my place about six, with dinner at seven. We'd be so happy if you came!"

His eyes twinkled gaily. "Certainly, Mrs. Moncrieff. I'm looking forward to it already."

The ne plus ultra of New Brewster society was impatiently assembled at the Moncrieff home shortly after 6, waiting to meet Mr. Hallinan, but it was not until 6:15 that he arrived. By then, thanks to Daisy Moncrieff's fearsome skill as a hostess, everyone present was equipped with a drink and with a set of speculations about the mysterious bachelor on the hill.

"I'm sure he must be a writer," said Martha Weede to liverish Dudley Heyer. "Daisy says he's tall and distinguished and just *radiates* personality. He's probably here only for a few months—just long enough to get to know us all, and then he'll write a novel about us."

"Hmm. Yes," Heyer said. He was an advertising executive who commuted to Madison Avenue every morning; he had an ulcer, and was acutely conscious of his role as a stereotype. "Yes, then he'll write a sizzling novel exposing suburban decadence, or a series of acid sketches for *The New Yorker*. I know the type."

Lys Erwin, looking desirable and just a bit disheveled after her third martini in thirty minutes, drifted by in time to overhear that. "You're *always* conscious of *types*, aren't you, darling? You and your gray flannel suit?"

Heyer fixed her with a baleful stare but found himself, as usual, unable to make an appropriate retort. He turned away, smiled hello at quiet little Harold and Jane Dewitt, whom he pitied somewhat (their son Lonny, age 9, was a shy, sensitive child, a total misfit among his playmates) and confronted the bar, weighing the probability of a night of acute agony against the immediate desirability of a Manhattan.

But at that moment Daisy Moncrieff reappeared

with Mr. Hallinan in tow, and conversation ceased abruptly throughout the parlor while the assembled guests stared at the newcomer. An instant later, conscious of their collective *faux pas,* the group began to chat again, and Daisy moved among her guests, introducing her prize.

"Dudley, this is Mr. Davis Hallinan. Mr. Hallinan, I want you to meet Dudley Heyer, one of the most talented men in New Brewster."

"Indeed? What do you do, Mr. Heyer?"

"I'm in advertising. But don't let them fool you; it doesn't take any talent at all. Just brass, nothing else. The desire to delude the public, and delude 'em good. But how about you? What line are you in?"

Mr. Hallinan ignored the question. "I've always thought advertising was a richly creative field, Mr. Heyer. But, of course, I've never really known at first hand—"

"Well, I have. And it's everything they say it is." Heyer felt his face reddening, as if he had had a drink or two. He was becoming talkative, and found Hallinan's presence oddly soothing. Leaning close to the newcomer, Heyer said, "Just between you and me, Hallinan, I'd give my whole bank account for a chance to stay home and *write*. Just write. I want to do a novel. But I don't have the guts; that's my trouble. I know that come Friday there's a $350 check waiting on my desk, and I don't dare give that up. So I keep writing my novel up here in my head, and it keeps eating me away down here in my gut. *Eating*." He paused, conscious that he had said too much and that his eyes were glittering beadily.

Hallinan wore a benign smile. "It's always sad to see talent hidden, Mr. Heyer. I wish you well."

Daisy Moncrieff appeared then, hooked an arm through Hallinan's, and led him away. Heyer, alone, stared down at the textured gray broadloom.

Now why did I tell him all that? he wondered. A minute after meeting Hallinan, he had unburdened his deepest woe to him—something he had not confided in anyone else in New Brewster, including his wife.

And yet—it had been a sort of catharsis, Heyer thought. Hallinan had calmly soaked up all his grief and inner agony, and left Heyer feeling drained and purified and warm.

Catharsis? Or a blood-letting? Heyer shrugged, then grinned and made his way to the bar to pour himself a Manhattan.

As usual, Lys and Leslie Erwin were at opposite ends of the parlor. Mrs. Moncrieff found Lys more easily, and introduced her to Mr. Hallinan.

Lys faced him unsteadily, and on a sudden impulse hitched her neckline higher. "Pleased to meet you, Mr. Hallinan. I'd like you to meet my husband Leslie. *Leslie!* Come here, please?"

Leslie Erwin approached. He was twenty years older than his wife, and was generally known to wear the finest pair of horns in New Brewster—a magnificent spread of antlers that grew a new point or two almost every week.

"Les, this is Mr. Hallinan. Mr. Hallinan, meet my husband, Leslie."

Mr. Hallinan bowed courteously to both of them. "Happy to make your acquaintance."

"The same," Erwin said. "If you'll excuse me, now—"

"The louse," said Lys Erwin, when her husband had returned to his station at the bar. "He'd sooner cut his throat than spend two minutes next to me in public." She glared bitterly at Hallinan. "I don't deserve that kind of thing, do I?"

Mr. Hallinan frowned sympathetically. "Have you any children, Mrs. Erwin?"

"Hah! He'd never give me any—not with *my* reputation! You'll have to pardon me; I'm a little drunk."

"I understand, Mrs. Erwin."

"I know. Funny, but I hardly know you and I like you. You seem to *understand*. Really, I mean." She took his cuff hesitantly. "Just from looking at you, I can tell you're not judging me like all the others. I'm not really *bad*, am I? It's just that I get so *bored*, Mr. Hallinan."

"Boredom is a great curse," Mr. Hallinan observed.

"Damn right it is! And Leslie's no help—always reading his newpapers and talking to his brokers! But I can't help myself, believe me." She looked around wildly. "They're going to start talking about us in a minute, Mr. Hallinan. Every time I talk to someone new they start whispering. But promise me something—"

"If I can."

"Someday—someday soon—let's get together? I want to *talk* to you. God, I want to talk to someone—someone who understands why I'm the way I am. Will you?"

"Of course, Mrs. Erwin. Soon." Gently he detached her hand from his sleeve, held it tenderly for a moment, and released it. She smiled hopefully at him. He nodded.

"And now I must meet some of the other guests. A pleasure, Mrs. Erwin."

He drifted away, leaving Lys weaving shakily in the

middle of the parlor. She drew in a deep breath and lowered her décolletage again.

At least there's one decent man in this town now, she thought. There was something *good* about Hallinan—good, and kind, and understanding.

Understanding. That's what I need. She wondered if she could manage to pay a visit to the house on Melon Hill tomorrow afternoon without arousing too much scandal.

Lys turned and saw thin-faced Aiken Muir staring at her slyly, with a clear-cut invitation on his face. She met his glance with a frigid, wordless *go to hell*.

Mr. Hallinan moved on, on through the party. And, gradually, the pattern of the party began to form. It took shape like a fine mosaic. By the time the cocktail hour was over and dinner was ready, an intricate, complex structure of interacting thoughts and responses had been built.

Mr. Hallinan, always drinkless, glided deftly from one New Brewsterite to the next, engaging each in conversation, drawing a few basic facts about the other's personality, smiling politely, moving on. Not until after he moved on did the person come to a dual realization: that Mr. Hallinan had said quite little, really, and that he had instilled a feeling of warmth and security in the other during their brief talk.

And thus while Mr. Hallinan learned from Martha Weede of her paralyzing envy of her husband's intelligence and of her fear of his scorn, Lys Erwin was able to remark to Dudley Heyer that Mr. Hallinan was a remarkably kind and understanding person. And Heyer, who had never been known to speak a kind word of anyone, for once agreed.

And later, while Mr. Hallinan was extracting from

Leslie Erwin some of the pain his wife's manifold infidelities caused him, Martha Weede could tell Lys Erwin, "He's so gentle—why, he's almost like a saint!"

And while little Harold Dewitt poured out his fear that his silent 9-year-old son Lonny was in some way subnormal, Leslie Erwin, with a jaunty grin, remarked to Daisy Moncrieff, "That man must be a psychiatrist. Lord, he knows how to talk to a person. Inside of two minutes he had me telling him all my troubles. I feel better for it, too."

Mrs. Moncrieff nodded. "I know what you mean. This morning, when I went up to his place to invite him here, we talked a little on his porch."

"Well," Erwin said, "if he's a psychiatrist he'll find plenty of business here. There isn't a person here riding around without a private monkey on his back. Take Heyer, over there—he didn't get that ulcer from happiness. That scatterbrain Martha Weede, too—married to a Columbia professor who can't imagine what to talk to her about. And my wife Lys is a very confused person too, of course."

"We all have our problems," Mrs. Moncrieff sighed. "But I feel much better since I spoke with Mr. Hallinan. Yes: *much* better."

Mr. Hallinan was now talking with Paul Jambell, the architect. Jambell, whose pretty young wife was in Springfield Hospital slowly dying of cancer. Mrs. Moncrieff could well imagine what Jambell and Mr. Hallinan were talking about.

Or rather, what Jambell was talking about—for Mr. Hallinan, she realized, did very little talking himself. But he was such a *wonderful* listener! She felt a pleasant glow, not entirely due to the cocktails. It was good to have someone like Mr. Hallinan in New Brewster, she thought. A man of his tact and dignity and warmth would be a definite asset.

When Lys Erwin woke—alone, for a change—the following morning, some of the past night's curious calmness had deserted her.

I have to talk to Mr. Hallinan, she thought.

She had resisted two implied and one overt attempts at seduction the night before, had come home, had managed even to be polite to her husband. And Leslie had been polite to her. It was most unusual.

"That Hallinan," he had said. "He's quite a guy."

"You talked to him too?"

"Yeah. Told him a lot. Too much, maybe. But I feel better for it."

"Odd," she said. "So do I. He's a strange one, isn't he? Wandering around that party, soaking up everyone's aches. He must have had half the neuroses in New Brewster unloaded on his back last night."

"Didn't seem to depress him, though. More he talked to people, more cheerful and affable he got. And us, too. You look more relaxed than you've been in a month, Lys."

"I *feel* more relaxed. As if all the roughness and ugliness in me was drawn out."

And that was how it had felt the next morning, too. Lys woke, blinked, looked at the empty bed across the room. Leslie was long since gone, on his way to the city. She knew she had to talk to Hallinan again. She hadn't got rid of it all. There was still some poison left inside her, something cold and chunky that would melt before Mr. Hallinan's warmth.

She dressed, impatiently brewed some coffee, and left the house. Down Copperbeech Road, past the Moncrieff house where Daisy and her stuffy husband Fred were busily emptying the ashtrays of the night before, down to Melon Hill and up the gentle slope to the split-level at the top.

Mr. Hallinan came to the door in a blue checked dressing gown. He looked slightly seedy, almost overhung, Lys thought. His dark eyes had puffy lids and a light stubble sprinkled his cheeks.

"Yes, Mrs. Erwin?"

"Oh—good morning, Mr. Hallinan. I—I came to see you. I hope I didn't disturb you—that you—that is—"

"Quite all right, Mrs. Erwin." Instantly she was at ease.

"But I'm afraid I am really extremely tired after last night, and I fear I shouldn't be very good company just now."

"But you said you'd talk to me alone today. And— oh, there's so much more I want to tell you!"

A shadow of feeling—*pain? fear?* Lys wondered— crossed his face. "No," he said hastily. "No more—not just yet. I'll have to rest today. Would you mind coming back—well, say Wednesday?"

"Certainly, Mr. Hallinan. I wouldn't want to disturb you."

She turned away and started down the hill, thinking: *he had too much of our troubles last night. He soaked them all up like a sponge, and today he's going to digest them—*

Oh, what am I thinking?

She reached the foot of the hill, brushed a couple of tears from her eyes, and walked home rapidly, feeling the October chill whistling around her.

And so the pattern of life in New Brewster developed.

For the six weeks before his death, Mr. Hallinan was a fixture at any important community gathering, always dressed impeccably, always ready with his cheerful smile, always uncannily able to draw forth whatever secret hungers and terrors lurked in his neighbors' souls.

And invariably Mr. Hallinan would be unapproachable in the day after these gatherings, would mildly but firmly turn away any callers. What he did, alone in the house on Melon Hill, no one knew. As the days passed, it occured to all that no one knew much of anything about Mr. Hallinan. He knew *them* all right, knew the one night of adultery twenty years before that still racked Daisy Moncrieff, knew the acid pain that seared Dudley Heyer, the cold envy glittering in Martha Weede, the frustration and loneliness of Lys Erwin, her husband's shy anger at his own cuckoldry—he knew these things and many more, but none of them knew more of him than his name.

Still, he warmed their lives and took from them the burden of their griefs. If he chose to keep his own life hidden, they said, that was his privilege.

He took walks every day, through still-wooded New Brewster, and would wave and smile to the children, who would wave and smile back. Occasionally he would stop, chat with a sulking child, then move on, tall, erect, walking with a jaunty stride.

He was never known to set foot in either of New Brewster's two churches. Once Lora Harker, a mainstay of the New Brewster Presbyterian Church, took him to task for this at a dull dinner party given by the Weedes.

But Mr. Hallinan smiled mildly and said, "Some of us feel the need. Others do not."

And that ended the discussion.

Toward the end of November a few members of the community experienced an abrupt reversal of their feelings about Mr. Hallinan—weary, perhaps, of his constant empathy for their woes. The change in spirit was spearheaded by Dudley Heyer, Carl Weede, and several of the other men.

"I'm getting not to trust that guy," Heyer said. He knocked dottle vehemently from his pipe, "Always hanging around soaking up gossip, pulling out dirt—and what the hell for? What does *he* get out of it?"

"Maybe he's practicing to be a saint," Carl Weede remarked quietly. "Self-abnegation. The Buddist Eightfold Path."

"The women all swear by him," said Leslie Erwin. "Lys hasn't been the same since he came here."

"*I'll* say she hasn't," said Aiken Muir wryly, and all of the men, even Erwin, laughed, getting the sharp thrust.

"All I know is I'm tired of having a father-confessor in our midst," Heyer said. "I think he's got a motive back of all his goody-goody warmness. When he's through pumping us he's going to write a book that'll put New Brewster on the map but good."

"You always suspect people of writing books," Muir said. *"Oh, that mine enemy would write a book! . . ."*

"Well, whatever his motives I'm getting annoyed. And that's why he hasn't been invited to the party we're giving on Monday night." Heyer glared at Fred Moncrieff as if expecting some dispute. "I've spoken to my wife about it, and she agrees. Just this once, dear Mr. Hallinan stays home."

It was strangely cold at the Heyers' party that Monday night. The usual people were there, unaware that

Mr. Hallinan had not been invited, waited expectantly for the chance to talk to him, and managed to leave early when they discovered he was not to be there.

"We should have invited him," Ruth Heyer said after the last guest had left.

Heyer shook his head. "No. I'm glad we didn't."

"But that poor man, all alone on the hill while the bunch of us were here, cut off from us. You don't think he'll get insulted, do you? I mean, and cut us from now on?"

"I don't care," Heyer said, scowling.

His attitude of mistrust toward Mr. Hallinan spread through the community. First the Muirs, then the Harkers, failed to invite him to gatherings of theirs. He still took his usual afternoon walks, and those who met him observed a slightly strained expression on his face, though he still smiled gently and chatted easily enough, and made no bitter comments.

And on December 3, a Wednesday, Roy Heyer, age 10, and Philip Moncrieff, age 9, set upon Lonny Dewitt, age 9, just outside the New Brewster Public School, just before Mr. Hallinan turned down the school lane on his stroll.

Lonny was a strange, silent boy, the despair of his parents and the bane of his classmates. He kept to himself, said little, nudged into corners and stayed there. People clucked their tongues when they saw him in the street.

Roy Heyer and Philip Moncrieff made up their minds they were going to make Lonny Dewitt say something, or else.

It was *or else*. They pummeled him and kicked him for a few minutes; then, seeing Mr. Hallinan approaching, they ran, leaving him weeping silently on the flagstone steps outside the empty school.

Lonny looked up as the tall man drew near.

"They've been hitting you, haven't they? I see them running away now."

Lonny continued to cry. He was thinking. *There's something funny about this man. But he wants to help me. He wants to be kind to me.*

"You're Lonny Dewitt, I think. Why are you crying? Come, Lonny, stop crying! They didn't hurt you that much."

They didn't, Lonny said silently. *I like to cry.*

Mr. Hallinan was smiling cheerfully. "Tell me all about it. Something's bothering you, isn't it? Something big, that makes you feel all lumpy and sad inside. Tell me about it, Lonny, and maybe it'll go away." He took the boy's small cold hands in his own, and squeezed them.

"Don't want to talk," Lonny said.

"But I'm a friend. I want to help you."

Lonny peered close and saw suddenly that the tall man told the truth. He wanted to help Lonny. More than that: he *had* to help Lonny. Desperately. He was pleading. "Tell me what's troubling you," Mr. Hallinan said again.

OK, Lonny thought. *I'll tell you.*

And he lifted the floodgates. Nine years of repression and torment came rolling out in one roaring burst.

I'm alone and they hate me because I do things in my head and they never understood and they think I'm queer and they hate me I see them looking funny at me and they think funny things about me because I want to talk to them with my mind and they can only hear words and I hate them hate them hate hate hate—

Lonny stopped suddenly. He had let it all out, and now he felt better, cleansed of the poison he'd been carrying in him for years. But Mr. Hallinan looked funny. He was pale and white-faced, and he was staggering.

In alarm, Lonny extended his mind to the tall man. And got:

Too much. Much too much. Should never have gone near the boy. But the older ones wouldn't let me.

Irony: the compulsive empath overloaded and burned out by a compulsive sender who'd been bottled up.

. . . like grabbing a high-voltage wire . . .

. . . he was a sender, I was a receiver, but he was too strong . . .

And four last bitter words: *I . . . was . . . a . . . leech. . . .*

"Please, Mr. Hallinan," Lonny said out loud. "Don't get sick. I want to tell you some more. Please Mr. Hallinan."

Silence.

Lonny picked up a final lingering wordlessness, and knew he had found and lost the first one like himself. Mr. Hallinan's eyes closed and he fell forward on his face in the street. Lonny realized that it was over, that he and the people of New Brewster would never talk to Mr. Hallinan again. But just to make sure he bent and took Mr. Hallinan's limp wrist.

He let go quickly. The wrist was like a lump of ice. *Cold*—burningly cold. Lonny stared at the dead man for a moment or two.

"Why, it's dear Mr. Hallinan," a female voice said. "Is he—"

And feeling the loneliness return, Lonny began to cry softly again.